A Virtue of Child

Justice #6

SUZAN HARDEN

This is a work of fiction. All characters, organizations and events in this novel are products of the author's imagination and are not to be construed as real. Any resemblance to persons, living or dead, is entirely coincidental.

A VIRTUE OF CHILD (Justice #6)
ISBN-13 - 978-1-938745-86-7
Copyright 2021 by Suzan Harden

Published by Angry Sheep Publishing
Findlay, Ohio

Cover Design by For the Muse Designs
Interior Design by JW Manus

To my grandmothers,
Eleanor and Marguerite,
for their love of books and reading

JUSTICE
(the novels)

Justice: The Beginning
A Question of Balance
A Modicum of Truth
A Matter of Death
A Touch of Mother
A Twist of Love
A Virtue of Child
A Hand of Father
A Measure of Knowledge

The Justice Thalia Stories

Snowfall

Murder Most Fowl

The Sweetest Poison

A Granddaughter of Mine

More Stories

Sword and Sorceress 28 ("Justice")

Sword and Sorceress 30 ("Diplomacy in the Dark")

For updates, news, and giveaways, join Suzan's mailing list or visit her website at www.suzanharden.com. You can also check her out on Twitter @Suzan_Harden or on Facebook at SuzanHardenWriter.

Prologue

Conflict's pursuit of Death and Her rejection of Him drove Conflict mad. He lashed out at everyone and everything, not realizing the harm He caused to the World, much less the harm He caused to Himself. Love feared if His insanity could not be healed, Balance and Light would banish Him for the final time.

Or worse, They would give Him to Death to destroy.

Once again, Love sought Her sister Child for advice, and Child said, "Borrow the chains Father forged for Light to capture Conflict. Grind the poppy seeds I give You and feed them to Conflict. Once He is asleep, bind Him in the chains and bring Him to Me.

So Love went to Father and asked to borrow the chains He forged to hold Conflict. "Why do You need such things, My Dear?" He asked.

"To capture a wild beast that ravages My garden." She held out Her hand to show Him Her sister's gift. "See? Child has already given Me seeds to grow new flowers. But I cannot plant them until I capture the beast and take him far away from My garden, else the beast will simply destroy My new flowers."

"But those chains are meant to hold one of Us," Father said.

"And since nothing is more powerful than the Twelve of Us, then I will have no problem capturing the beast and relocating him far from My garden," Love replied.

Father could not deny Her logic, so He gave the chains to Love, and She invited Conflict to visit Her.

Conflict accepted Her invitation eagerly, believing She had forgiven Him and They would once again lay together.

When Conflict arrived at Love's garden, He found She had laid out a magnificent feast for Him. She plied Him with rich foods and fine wines. For dessert, She served Him sweet cakes made with the poppy seeds. The seeds caused Him to fall into a stupor. She bound Him in Father's chains, and She carried Him to Child.

Much later, Conflict awoke to find Love gone and Himself bound and lying in Child's bed. She watched Him with a sorrowful expression. He threatened and roared and thrashed, but He could not break free from the chains.

"How could You and Love do this to Me, Sister?" He cried.

"Brother, I merely want You to see the damage You wrought," Child said gently. "Love fears for Your existence, and You will surely destroy Yourself if You continue in Your pursuit of Death. Or You will force Us to destroy You to preserve the World."

She gently cupped His cheek and concentrated. Her mind melded with His. Since She felt the joy and the pain of all the World's creatures, from the largest whale to the tiniest seed, He felt it, too. Together, They wept and Their tears washed the agony from the World.

– The Seventh Book of Child, Verses III thru XVI

Chapter 1

I jerked out of an unsound sleep, a scream at the back of my throat from the nightmare. There was no one and nothing in my bedchambers that shouldn't be. My legs were tangled in the single sheet of cotton I used, and it was damp from my cold sweat. Part of me wished Luc was here to hold me, reassure me even though we both knew it was a lie.

He hadn't slept in my bed since his child died. Since the night my birth mother plunged her knife into Sister Claudia's womb. Gerd planned to use the babe's death to fuel an obscene spell to rip open a gateway for the demons to enter our realm. I didn't blame Luc for avoiding me. I'd horribly underestimated my mother, and he couldn't look at me without seeing her.

Claudia had visited me once. She was now as barren as I was. Master Aaron couldn't heal or replace what the demon magic my mother wielded had corrupted. My meeting with Claudia was awkward. She claimed she didn't blame me. However I blamed myself enough for the three of us.

I unwrapped the sheet from my limbs. There was no point in trying to go back to sleep. A few candlemarks a night was all the rest I could manage over the last two months before nightmares of my headless mother and Luc and Claudia's bloody babe intruded.

From the silence in the corridor outside my chamber door, we were nowhere near First Morning. Whispers came from the new passage I'd created to the tunnel system, the passage hidden by my wardrobe. I ignored them as I climbed out of bed and searched for a loose shirt and pants to wear.

Once dressed and my hair tied back out of the way, I padded through the silent Temple. Warden Tahoma nodded as we passed on his patrol, but otherwise, we said nothing. All of the Balance wardens took my idiosyncrasies in stride, just as they did with my fellow justices, Yanaba and Elizabeth.

I passed through the Temple kitchen to the back porch. Our cook Deborah and her kitchen staff weren't even awake yet. The hearth and the brick oven glowed a dark pink, their fires stoked for the night.

In the exercise yard, I went through warm-ups and stretches before I started on the Jing unarmed combat forms Sister Shi Hua of Light had started to teach me before she also became pregnant.

I went through the first set and started on the second when I felt someone's attention on me. The yellow tomato vines climbing the wooden lattice work of the garden couldn't hide the small figure with the bright orange face and hands. I frowned.

"Ming Wei, what are you doing up this late?" I cocked my head. "Or rather, this early?"

Yanaba's squire cautiously peered around the corner of the wood frame. "I couldn't sleep."

"Nightmares?" I asked.

She nodded. The girl had more of a right to bad dreams than any of us. Her parents had sold her to a Jing noble located here in Issura. A noble who ill-used her before he burned his manse with himself and his child slaves inside. Ming Wei had been the only survivor.

With my strange eyesight, I couldn't see the awful scars and distorted flesh on the left side of her face and body, so I didn't stare at her like everyone else did. It was one of things that made her semi-comfortable around me. It also said something about her strength that she survived the horrible damage.

"May I say something?" she asked shyly.

"Of course."

"You need to keep your back foot pointed forward," she whispered. It was the same weakness Shi Hua had noticed and commented on.

I cocked my head. "You know these forms?"

"Yes, m'lady."

Now, I was thoroughly confused. "Where did you learn them?"

"Mistress Yin Li has been teaching me along with her son."

"During your language lessons?" I gaped at the child.

Ming Wei nodded. "Are you angry, m'lady? Justice Yanaba said it was all right for me to learn and share my knowledge with Nathan."

"I am . . . surprised." And I was. Ambassador Quan and his alleged mistress had been going to the Temple of Light the last few months. Since Shi Hua was a distance speaker, it was easier for them to go there to communicate with the emperor in Jing due to the sister being past the middle of her pregnancy. Few outside of the ambassador's small circle knew his alleged mistress was in fact the ambassador's bodyguard and Shi Hua's maternal aunt. Even fewer knew Yin Li was a priestess of Love.

Yanaba had encouraged her squire to relearn the Jing language, something the child refused to speak since the night she was rescued. Plus, Ming Wei's presence gave Yin Li's son someone to socialize with.

"Do you think Mistress Yin Li would allow Nathan to join you for your lessons?" I asked.

"If you requested it, I'm sure she would." The girl nodded solemnly.

"Do you think you could assist me with my second level forms?"

Her color brightened, and waves of anxiety rolled off her. "You want me to teach you?"

I shrugged. "Sister Shi Hua started teaching me, but she cannot continue until after her baby is born. I don't want to forget everything she has taught me so far, so I'd greatly appreciate your assistance."

Despite her jitters, Ming Wei bowed. "I would be honored, m'lady."

Ming Wei and I stopped our practice when the kitchen girls arrived to begin their work. While they proceeded to collect eggs from our henhouse, Deborah stepped out onto the porch and gave Ming Wei a honeyed treat before I sent the child off to the communal bathing room the female wardens used. When I followed my cook and Yanaba's squire into the kitchen, Deborah waited until the child raced down the hallway before she turned, scowled at me, and shook her spoon in my face.

"What are you thinking, Chief Justice?" Deborah waved the wooden utensil dramatically. I was rather thankful she was not holding a knife. "Keeping that poor girl up half the night! Justice Yanaba actually depends on her squire, even if you don't need young Nathan to the same level."

"I didn't keep her up," I snapped. "I couldn't sleep so I went to the practice yard. She was in the garden. watching me, so I invited her to help me work on the Jing fighting forms."

As I talked, Deborah strode over to the cupboard, placed her spoon on her work table, and pulled out leftover sourdough bread and hard cheese. She retrieved a knife and sliced both and placed them on a plate.

"Ming Wei said she is still having nightmares," I finished softly. "That's why she was awake and sitting in the garden."

"We know, m'lady." Deborah wiped her hands on her apron before she brought the plate over and gently pushed me toward the table in the little nook her assistants used for prep work. "The wardens on night watch keep an eye out for her. Dezba is the only one who can approach her without frightening the child."

That made sense. Dezba was a tiny woman, but she could be as fierce or as gentle as a situation called for. Her smaller stature and her gender would be less threatening to the child.

"Hasn't Yanaba been sending her to Brother Turtle?" I asked before I bit into the bread. To me, the priest qualified as a miracle worker after he saved my junior justice's life when she over-extended her spirit in her efforts to save the city from a demon attack last spring.

"Sort of . . ." Deborah shook her head. "The child has had so much trauma inflicted on her in her short life. She fears Brother Turtle after—" She sighed. "High Sister Mya has taken over Ming Wei's care, but not even she can heal such emotional wounds in half a year."

I nodded, tore a slice of cheese into bite-size pieces, and chewed as I analyzed the situation while Deborah bustled around the kitchen. She was right. And I couldn't even begin to comprehend what had been done to Ming Wei, much less how she had the strength to survive it. When I finished eating, I placed my plate in the tub for used kitchenware.

"I don't know what we'd do without you, Deborah." I hugged the older woman. For the first time, it truly registered how frail she was. She'd been the cook here before my grandmother Thalia was chief justice of Orrin. And I was hardly a child at thirty-one winters.

Deborah patted my hand. "No offense meant, but you need a bath yourself, Chief Justice."

I laughed and headed for my quarters.

After bathing and changing, I strode down to my office, took a seat in my chair, and started reviewing the pile of cases I'd failed to deal with in a timely manner. My junior justice had been handling court hearings, but Yanaba was more than halfway through her pregnancy. We'd already lost one potential Light child. Everyone was doting on

Yanaba, including me. And it was well past time I began performing my own duties again.

No sooner than that thought had passed through my head when someone pounded on my door. "Chief Justice?"

Warden Mylon's voice. I rarely saw the man. He preferred the night watch.

"Come in," I called out.

He opened the door and peered around the edge. "The magistrate wishes to see you."

Orrin's magistrate Malven DiCook pushed past the warden. Rather than taking DiCook's brusqueness in stride as most of Balance's guards would have done, Mylon grabbed DiCook's arm and swung him until he was pinned against the wall with Mylon's knife at his throat.

Let's just say there was a reason my chief warden acceded to Mylon's wish for the night shift.

"Anthea?" DiCook squeaked.

"Warden, please release the magistrate," I said. "The duke would be most vexed with me if you slit the magistrate's throat, even by accident."

"Yes, Lady Justice." Mylon released DiCook with a scowl. "Next time, wait until you're invited inside." He stalked out of my office and pulled the door quietly shut behind him.

"You let your wardens get away with too much," DiCook grumbled as he straightened his jacket. His extra clothing was necessary. The nights were finally becoming cooler as we approached the Vintner's Festival. The summer had been unusually hot, and everyone in Orrin welcomed the respite.

"And you presume too much, so the contest is even," I shot back. "I suggest not trying Warden Mylon's patience again." I gentled my tone. "What are you doing here at this hour? Surely you aren't that desperate for a decent meal."

The fact that the magistrate often showed up at meal times had become something of a running joke among my staff. But after tasting his wife's culinary skills myself, I totally understood why he came to Balance or Light for food.

"Remember Dante and Barbora's shop?"

A chill ran through me. Dante was one of DiCook's top peacekeepers. Or had been until he and his family were murdered to feed the demon eggs planted inside their bodies. Dante's wife Barbora ran a seamstress shop, and the family lived in the apartment on the second floor. We tried to locate any family members, but we came up empty-handed, so I signed off on the duchy taking possession of the property.

"I thought it was sold at the monthly magistrate's sale."

"It was." DiCook hooked his thumbs in his belt and rocked on his heels. My gut clenched at his sign that I wasn't going to like what I heard.

"The new owner opened up the storefront this morning for the first time." DiCook shrugged. "What she thought was a dead animal inside turned out to be human corpses."

Chapter 2

I cursed and leaned back in my chair. The demon voices whispered excitedly in the back of my head. However, I ignored them and focused on the magistrate. "How many and how long have they been there?"

"We're not sure how many bodies exactly," he said. "It's a mess. They've been in the shop two to four days from the decay. I've already sent for Master Healer Bly."

I didn't have to ask why he needed me. I rose, donned my formal robes and buckled on my sword harness.

"Have you sent a messenger to Light?" I asked.

"Peacekeeper Leyti will meet us on the street with a priest."

I didn't want to ask, but I did anyway when the magistrate didn't mention a priest's name. "He's been drinking again?" I wasn't referring to the peacekeeper.

DiCook sighed. He didn't ask who I meant. "According to Brother Garbhan, the high brother stops long enough to piss and pass out."

I frowned. "What do you mean 'according to Brother Garbhan'?"

"I've been added to the list of people banned from the Temple of Light." The magistrate shrugged. Unfortunately, it was within Luc's purview as the head of Orrin's Temple of Light to ban any civilian who disrupted the Temple's daily business. I didn't have any doubt DiCook had words with Luc about his drinking, and that was the real reason the magistrate had been barred from Light.

"What about Jeremy and Shi Hua?" I asked. "What do they say?"

"Brother Jeremy says nothing to me. His loyalty to Luc is absolute." DiCook followed me out of my office. "And I can't speak to Sister Shi Hua because Chief Healer Aaron has put her on bedrest, so she hasn't left the Temple at all."

I jerked to a halt in the corridor. "Bed rest? Is there something wrong—"

DiCook raised his right palm. "It's a precaution. Mistress Yin Li mentioned some issues Shi Hua's mother had experienced in her pregnancies. When Shi Hua exhibited similar symptoms, Aaron erred on the side of caution since she's definitely carrying a Light child."

I continued walking toward the courtroom. "He's certain her babe is Light?"

"Says so." DiCook chuckled. "It's not like I have any blessed talent to confirm a Twelve-damned thing."

We entered the sanctuary/courtroom of Balance as he finished his comment. Two of my wardens waited with a peacekeeper.

Warden Noko scowled at DiCook. "Language, Magistrate. Just because the chief justice has no sense of decorum, it doesn't mean you should follow in her footsteps."

I glared at the normally quiet woman. However, Warden Gina and the peacekeeper snickered. As usual, the basalt statue of Balance said nothing.

"Forgive me, Lady Warden." DiCook bowed to Noko. "I shall endeavor to keep the chief justice's poor manners from influencing my own. In the meantime, can we deal with the possible crimes discovered by a poor shopkeeper this morning?"

The magistrate, our bodyguards, and I exited the Temple of Balance. It was a shame DiCook and I as city leaders could no longer walk through the streets of Orrin without an escort. Between demon attacks and human renegades, no one took chances these days.

I could no longer even walk to Bakers Street on the days we didn't have court. It was the people watching I missed as much as the delicious puff pastries. Now, I had to look at nearly every citizen as a potential assassin.

Brother Garbhan and Warden Yar waited for us at the bottom of the steps leading up to my Temple with Peacekeeper Leyti. The three men nodded politely and greeted us, but as I got closer to the men, the acidic smell of vomit met my nose. Following the odor, I looked up at Yar. He merely gave a slight shake of his head, his expression begging me not to say anything.

Truly, there was nothing to say. Luc was by no means a short man, but Yar was a giant by comparison. And if my love was a dead weight from passing out drunk, it would take someone of the warden's size to wrestle him into bed.

Nor was this the first time the staff of Light had to deal with a drink-addicted chief priest.

Were Luc and I doomed to repeat my maternal grandparents' mistakes?

Luckily, the deceased seamstress's shop was a short walk from the Temple District. Along with two peacekeepers securing the building, several women were gathered around the entrance to the storefront. One in particular leaned against the stone wall of the first story. Her eyes were closed, and a pained expression etched lines across her delicate features.

The women's murmuring stopped as we walked up to the shop. One of them edged closer to the leaning woman and said, "The chief justice is here, Jaci."

Her eyes popped open, and she straightened and bowed. "Chief Justice, Brother. Thank you for coming."

She spoke with a bit of an accent I couldn't quite place.

"When did you get possession of the keys to this shop, Mistress Jaci?" I asked.

"First Day of last week. I paid the magistrate's clerk after the auction, and she gave me the keys." She hugged herself. "I waited until all of my sisters and nieces arrived in Orrin before I came over to the shop."

I turned to DiCook.

"I already confirmed the account with my clerk that Mistress Jaci received the keys eight days ago, Chief Justice." DiCook scowled, but I had the impression he was more disturbed by his memories of Dante and what we'd found here last winter. "She's available for whenever you need to truthspell her."

"Truthspell?" The woman who brought Jaci's attention to my presence shook, but from the red of her exposed skin, it was anger, not fear that provoked her. She also had the same unrecognizable accent. "We're the aggrieved parties!"

"Calm, Maiara," Jaci said sternly. "The chief justice is the reason you and my nieces are alive."

"You don't have an Issuran or Cantan accent." I cocked my head. "Were you in Tandor during the demon siege?"

"I wasn't, Lady Justice." A wan smile crossed Jaci's face. "My sister Maiara and her family were." She waved toward the angry woman. "Her husband and her eldest daughter's wife were lost during the defense of the city. As for our accents, our parents were part of the Tupi Forest Guardians. They immigrated to Issura based on their High Sister of Vintner's recommendation to assist the Duke of Tandor with his medicinal garden."

"The Valley of the Lost is very different from the Southern Long Continent's Great Forest," I said.

"Mother said that stark contrast is one of the reasons they stayed in Tandor. However—" Jaci gestured at the door. "We hoped to reopen the seamstress shop to give Maiara and her daughters an occupation and an income. Our youngest sister Moema's daughters have been apprenticing with me over the summer. Moema arrived yesterday from Redwood Grove to help us clean, organize, and inventory the shop."

"Inventory?" I asked.

"The duke ordered me to include all of Barbora's fabrics, thread, tools, and so on," DiCook offered. "Part of the sale money will go back to Mistress Jaci and her family to complete the orders Barbora never finished."

Of course, Duke Marco would. He had been trying very hard to be equitable to his people since he inherited the duchy. The sudden influx of refugees from our sister city of Tandor had made his position a delicate balancing act.

One that hadn't been helped by the year's spate of murders.

"Has there been any reports of missing people in the city?" I asked.

"No." DiCook grinned. "After your little tantrum a few months ago, even the folks in the South Side are talking to a few of the peacekeepers now. Closest we came was a young couple who tried to talk High Mother Leocadia into marrying them."

I tried not to think about that day I lost control. Tensions had spilled over between the unusual heat, the murders Leocadia's predecessor Bianca ordered to cover up her child selling, and the massive number of Tandoran refugees who were blamed for the murders. Somehow, I produced lightning. It was not a typical Balance talent, and I hadn't been able to replicate it since, but maybe that was a good thing.

"I take it the two are underage?" I asked.

"Yes," DiCook confirmed amicably. "Turns out both sets of parents merely wanted them to wait until their majority before they wed. The children took the request as forbidding them from being together."

"Magistrate, when was the last time any of your people entered the shop?" I couldn't bring myself to say Dante or Barbora's names. It was bad enough the voices in my head crooned over the loss of the eggs implanted in the couple and their children's bodies.

DiCook stroked his beard. "Peacekeeper Jaime and his team did the official inventory for the magistrate's sale a week and a half ago."

"I'm assuming they made no mention of any bodies."

"No, Chief Justice. It was two days before the sale."

Brother Garbhan hadn't said a word so far. Times like these were when I missed Luc the most. I'd come to depend on his calm demeanor and his strength.

"I'll need to question them as well."

"Of course, Chief Justice."

"And if you would be so kind, collect the names of all of Mistress Jaci's family members present and where they are staying." I turned my attention to the group of women and pushed back my hood. Their shudders and gestures to ward bad luck meant my red eyes had their desired effect. "I don't think I need to say none of you may leave Orrin until I speak to you. As the magistrate and Brother Garbhan can attest, I am rarely in a generous mood, and I am even less so when I don't have the chance to drink my morning tea."

All of the women murmured their agreement, except Jaci who smiled and nodded. She seemed relieved someone else was commanding her sisters. Her attitude made me wonder how often she had to mediate family tempers.

I turned to the door. The key was still sitting in the locking mechanism. I drew one of my smaller knives and slid the steel between the door and the jamb. The door was still unlocked, which attested to the women's haste in leaving the shop.

Under different circumstances, I could retrieve residual skin or hair from the door latch. It may be a moot point with Jaci and her family touching the metal, but I would stick to my established procedures.

With my elbow, I pushed the wood as I used my knife to raise the lever. The door creaked open. The smell slapped me so hard I gagged. Behind me Brother Garbhan coughed and choked. Then came the splash of his first meal of the day on the street cobblestones.

"You might want to let the building air out, Lady Justice," one of the peacekeepers volunteered.

"We're going to need a wind talent with more power than a Peaceful Sea fall storm to clear out this smell," I muttered. The voices in the back of my mind relished the odor of death, which only made my stomach roil more. It was a good thing I'd eaten earlier than normal. Otherwise, I'd be joining Garbhan and expelling Deborah's excellent bread onto the street.

There was nothing but materials and body forms in the front of the shop. I touched the corner of a work counter. Everything was as it had been since the last time I was in here, other than a thick layer of dust, which tickled the inside of my nose.

I followed the Balance-awful scent to the back living quarters. Hot yellow maggots slithered through the body parts piled on what had been Barbora's dining table. Flies and other scavenging insects took flight at our entrance, causing streaks of red light in my odd vision, before quickly settling back down to their feast.

"What in Light's infinite names—" Garbhan's voice was muffled. I peered over my right shoulder. He had placed a fold of his cloak over his mouth and nose. I couldn't blame him. This was far beyond his previous duties as an aide to the Reverend Father of Light in Standora.

"Is it just my peculiar sight, or is that a pile of limbs with no torsos or heads?" I asked.

"It's not you—" The poor priest twisted to his right and proceeded to lose whatever was left in his stomach onto the dusty wooden floorboards.

Chapter 3

"Are you sure you want to continue?" I asked Garbhan. "One of my wardens can handle the witnessing."

The brother sat on the tail of the Healers Guild wagon and sipped a drought Master Healer Bly had given him to settle his stomach. His skin returned to pale yellow, which was much better than the greenish hue he wore when I helped him out of the shop.

More citizens of Orrin had gathered around the shop. So far, it was curiosity. I prayed to Light to please keep them peaceful. I couldn't handle another riot. I could not risk losing control.

The voices from the demon grimoire offered to show me how to control the lightning. I gritted my teeth and focused on the priest next to me.

"No, Lady Justice." Garbhan gulped more of the medicine. "Master Bly's potion is doing its job. Besides—" He smiled weakly. "—I don't think there's anything left in me to vomit."

Bly exited the shop, followed by Master Healer Devin. At the peace-keeper's initial report of multiple bodies, he had accompanied her so she would have an extra pair of hand. Bly's intern Simi was the last to come out.

Unfortunately, the young woman's color was the same greenish shade Garbhan's had been. She whirled away from the crowd and ran for the alley. She didn't quite make it before she lost the contents of her stomach.

The two senior healers gathered their equipment to take samples for both themselves and me. If the people whose limbs lay inside in the dining table fought back against whoever killed them, there might be some of their murderer's skin or blood in their fingernails if the insects hadn't consumed the soft debris. Bly glanced at me as both she and Devin dabbed on ointment under their noses and tied on masks to deal with the odor of rotten flesh while they worked.

"In a way, I'm glad it's not just me getting sick," the Light priest whispered.

"It's not just you," I whispered back. "The only reason the master healers and I didn't get sick is we've seen worse things."

"The ointment helps, too," Bly mock-whispered, which prompted some titters from the closer members for the crowd.

Blood rushed to Garbhan's cheeks, shifting his skin to an orange-red. "I meant no disrespect, m'ladies."

I patted his shoulder. "There's nothing to apologize for. I hope to the Twelve you never see some of the desecration we have."

My words seemed to be the right thing to say. Garbhan's shoulder relaxed beneath my touch.

He looked around us, but the peacekeepers and wardens kept the fishwives back from the shop. His attention return to me, but he still kept his voice low. "I hope my reports to the Reverend Father make him realize what Orrin is dealing with. These things aren't happening in Standora."

No one in the capital, except maybe Crown Princess Chiara, was taking the events in Orrin and Tandor seriously. But then, she led the Queen's army in the Battle of Tandor. Finding yourself face-to-face with one demon, much less an entire army of them, generally made one a believer.

"I'm going to give you the same lecture I gave Justice Yanaba, Brother Jeremy, and my own wardens." I squeezed Garbhan's shoulder. "We do not guess. We do not assume. We follow the evidence."

"Yes, m'lady," he murmured.

"And on that note, I want Warden Noko to witness for me."

"B-but—" Garbhan stared up at me. "I assure you I can do my duty as your witness—"

"This isn't about your skill or devotion to duty." I tried to keep a reassuring expression on my face. "We can't afford to lose any more Light clergy. If this is another trap, I don't want you anywhere near me when I start the rewind." I grinned. "Besides, Sister Cedar Grove would be most vexed if I got you killed."

His skin glowed orange, and his eyes widened. "You, uh, she, um . . ."

"I'm merely glad you're making friends." I scanned the crowd as we spoke. "It's difficult being transferred from a prominent post to a backwater city."

"Orrin is not a backwater," he protested.

"I'm glad you think so," I said agreeably.

He sputtered a bit more before Warden Gina leaned close to him and said, "She's teasing you, Brother."

"Oh." He gulped.

Gina straightened and faced me with a frown. "And you need to stop, m'lady. He's not the high brother."

I probably teased Garbhan about his relationship with Thief's second to avoid thinking about my own problems. I was the first to know Cedar Grove was pregnant with Garbhan's child thanks to the peculiar sight I cursed myself with when I tried to cure my blindness. Still, it wasn't fair to the young priest. Many of those in Balance and Light found the recent proclamation to procreate uncomfortable.

"I apologize, Brother." I inclined my head. "Inappropriate humor is my own mechanism for dealing with terrible situations."

He gulped again before he said, "I understand your reasoning, Chief Justice, but I'll never have the experience the city needs if you and the high brother don't train me."

His unspoken accusation sent a shiver through me. So Luc was ignoring the newest member of his temple. That was definitely not a good sign.

Gina grimaced. She would never say a word about someone outside of Balance, but her expression meant there was more going on than the news DiCook had told me when he arrived at my Temple. I would definitely need to have a private conversation with her and my chief warden once we were done here. In the meantime, I would have to see to Garbhan's investigative training despite my reservations about putting his life in danger.

Masters Devin and Bly exited the seamstress shop once again. After setting their equipment and samples in their wagon, Bly pulled her mask from her face.

"We've got the initial samples we knew you'd request, Chief Justice." She inclined her head toward the building. "Do you want the body parts removed before you do the rewind?"

"As much as I want to, no." I eyed Bly. "If you don't mind, could Warden Noko, Brother Garbhan, and I have some of your nose ointment before we go in?"

"Of course." She smiled.

While we applied ointment and covered our lower faces with clean silk handkerchiefs we normally used to collect potential evidence, Master Devin stepped closer to me.

"Are you coming to the Guild House to observe?"

I nodded. It wasn't like I really had a choice in the matter.

"Then we'll speak when there's not so many ears around."

A chill ran through me. Devin was one to always speak his mind, regardless of who was nearby. Did he notice something with the limbs piled on the table that neither Brother Garbhan nor I had?

"Very well." I turned to Noko and Garbhan. "Ready?"

"Yes, m'lady," my warden promptly replied.

Garbhan's skin around his eyes shifted to a greenish yellow.

I lowered my voice. "You don't have to come."

He straightened his spine despite his ghastly skin color and the green beads of sweat developing on his forehead. "I will do my duty, Chief Justice."

I nodded before I pivoted and strode back inside the shop. The ointment helped a little, but it couldn't completely block or disguise the scent of rotten flesh.

"How do you wish to proceed, Chief Justice?" Noko asked. Other than Gina, she was the best non-priest who witnessed for me. Before we left Balance, I had decided to give her a bit more experience. I really hoped she didn't think I was punishing her by asking for her assistance in this matter.

"Justice Yanaba?" I said both aloud and silently.

Yes, Chief Justice.

"Have you started court yet?"

No, m'lady. Is there something you require?

"Have Justice Elizabeth preside over today's cases. I need your assistance."

Yanaba's laughter tinkled like silver bells in my mind. *How many blocks this time?*

"It's only one building. Barbora's seamstress shop and apartment."

I felt Yanaba's sudden intake of breath. She'd nearly killed herself dealing with the murders of Barbora and her family because I'd been ordered to investigate the Temple of Balance in Tandor.

If this is too much for you or the baby . . . I said resorting solely to silent speech.

No, she whispered in my mind. *Just old nightmares.* I felt her exhale through the link before my skin tingled with her magic. *What specifically do you want me to do?*

"We're going to rewind the events in the building," I said aloud again. "Unfortunately, the last known time we know no bodies were in here was eleven days ago."

Yanaba swore a few colorful oaths. *No wonder you want help. Give me a moment to inform Elizabeth.* Her presence receded. I counted my breaths. At twenty-four, Yanaba's mind touched mine again. *All right. Any chance a trap spell has been set on these bodies?*

I laughed. "These days, I'd be disappointed if there wasn't."

I am ready.

I turned my attention to Noko and Garbhan. "Brother, be ready if there is a trap spell or any other nasty magic."

He nodded.

"Warden, you'll observe the front room." I pointed to the tiny narrow staircase. "You'll also follow if anyone goes up the stairs." I lowered my arm. "Brother, you'll stay here in the living quarters."

They both answered, "Yes, m'lady."

I crossed to the southern wall and sat cross-legged on the dusty floor, facing the stones. Sivan would chide me for getting my clothing filthy, but it couldn't be helped. The best substance to pull the memories of the last eleven days would be the sea- and river-washed rocks forming the first story's walls.

Placing my bare palms on the polished surfaces, I concentrated. With Yanaba's help, I yanked the timelines back past the necessary time period. I let the strings slip through my fingers at a certain rate. A day passed.

From the front room, Noko called out, "Nothing. Nothing. Nothing. Slower, m'lady!"

Perspiration broke out on my forehead at the effort to curb the flow even with Yanaba's help.

"Jaime has entered with two men and a woman," Noko reported. From her clear voice, she stood near the doorway to the front shop. "All four are dressed in city peacekeeping uniforms. Two of them go into the living quarters. Jaime and one of the men start going through the seamstress's equipment and supplies. Jaime is comparing what's in the room with a scroll he's carrying."

That would be the copy of the list of Dante and Barbora's belongings I had delivered to the magistrate's office after their deaths. It was good to know DiCook was being thorough in his duties.

Garbhan picked up the recitation. "The other man and the woman come into the living quarters. She waves toward the staircase, and they proceed up the steps." Wood creaked as the Light priest followed the ghosts of the past to the second story. He and Noko ignored my orders, but I couldn't berate them properly without dropping the spell.

"They are also cross-checking what is up here versus the inventory your Temple provided," Garbhan shouted.

I let time speed up just a bit. A few heartbeats later, bootsteps came back down the steps.

"The two I followed are finishing their inventory of personal property in this room," Garbhan added. "Now, they head back into the shop area."

"Peacekeeper Jaime asks the other pair something," Noko continued. "They both nod. All four are leaving."

Nothing interesting or unusual so far, but I didn't expect otherwise from Jaime. He was a quiet, shy man, but very conscientious in the performance of his duties.

I let the strings of time slip faster through my fingers. One day passed. Two. Three. Four.

"Hold!" Garbhan's shout nearly made me lose my control of the spell. It was night at this pause.

"Warden, get in here!" he called sternly.

It was rare for Garbhan to show his true nature. He'd adapted a quiet, unassuming personality in order to keep an eye on Issura's Reverend Father of Light for the Reverend Father of Thief. As much as I hated politics, there was a growing body of circumstantial evidence Reverend Father Farrell may be connected to the renegades. He definitely hadn't made a good impression on anyone at Love with his obsession for the younger priestesses.

Bootsteps pounded into the living room, and Noko gasped. "What in Balance's thousand names!"

"Witness!" I demanded. Holding time in place strained my resources as well as Yanaba's.

"I'm drawing in the dust," Garbhan answered. "We're going to need your clerks to draft a better picture. Something not human came through the back door. I think it picked the back lock because I don't see any damage to the door."

"The creature walks upright," Noko said. "It appears like a Wildling caught halfway in their change. Furred. Long talons, but it still has thumbs. The head—" She paused, obviously searching for the right words. "Prominent ears. Long snout. It doesn't quite resemble a bear or a wolf. Something . . . in between. And it has the horns of a white-tailed deer. It's carrying an intact body. A woman."

"I can't hold the lines forever," I said through gritted teeth. Sweat soaked through my small clothes and dampened my silk tunic.

"Go," Garbhan said.

Time eased forward under my grip. Noko took up the recitation while Garbhan tried to capture the perpetrator's appearance.

"It lays the body on the table. It—" She choked and coughed. "It uses its talons to rip open the body and starts eating the internal organs."

She made gagging noises before she added, "The creature seems to be relishing the heart the most."

"Go outside, Warden," Garbhan murmured. "Get some fresh air."

"B-but—"

"Go on, Noko," I ground out. "Before I get sick myself from hearing you retch."

"Yes, m'lady." She sounded on the verge of tears. From the rhythm of the floorboards beneath me and the pounding of her boots, she ran from the living area. I couldn't allow myself any sympathy for the woman.

Not yet anyway. My limbs started to tremble of the exertion of the spell.

"The creature rips off the head of the corpse, and it eats the brains," Garbhan continued grimly. At least, he didn't sound like he was about to get sick again, too. "It tears off the arms and the legs."

"Was the woman clothed?" My words were punctuated by little gasps, and I blinked sweat from my eyes.

"No." Garbhan sounded puzzled. "It collects the remains of the torso and skull, and it leaves, but it doesn't touch the limbs."

I could feel Yanaba listening through me, and she was just as confused. However, we needed more information. I started to speed the timeline. Nearly a day passed.

"Slow," Garbhan barked. My shoulders and back ached, but I did as he said. I could feel the creature's timing was around First Night, the same as before.

"It brings in another woman. Again either unconscious or dead. No clothing. The creature performs the same ritual of eating the innards." The priest paused before he added, "And the brains."

I let time flow at a sedate pace through my fingers. There had to be a clue here in the creature's actions.

"Again, it removes the limbs before collecting the torso and skull.

Chief Justice . . ." Garbhan hesitated. "It almost appears as if the creature is using the limbs to create a design on the table."

He reported two more women devoured and dismembered over the course of two more nights before he said, "This is new. A male youth."

"Young enough to be mistaken as female?" I asked.

"Or possibly *berda*," Garbhan replied. "Without any clothing, it's difficult to tell how he originally appeared." Another pause filled the air. "This time, it is eating the heart first. I'm sketching the layers of the limbs. I recognize a couple of the symbols. If I'm right, this creature is leaving someone a message. Or possibly casting a spell."

"Why here?" I murmured more to myself than to the young priest.

"The demon eggs? The family's deaths?" Garbhan chuckled softly. "You're the one who preaches that we shouldn't jump to conclusions."

This all happened on consecutive nights, Yanaba whispered in my mind at the same time Garbhan said the words aloud. My junior justice sounded as tired as I felt. *Why didn't anyone notice this thing?* she added.

"I can't hold the timelines too much longer, Brother," I said.

"One moment," he pleaded. His fingernail scraped against wood as fast as if he were using a stick of charcoal. "I have it. Go."

Time flowed faster through my grip.

"Nothing, but the increase of insect activity," Garbhan reported. "A family of rats have come in and are feasting on the flesh along with the flies and maggots. The rats' motions through the pile result in the shifting and jumble of the limbs."

Time oozed into the present. I groaned at the cramping of my major muscles along with a good number of little ones. DiCook's estimate of how long the limbs had been rotting in here was only a few days off. I didn't expect total accuracy from him, but he'd obviously picked up quite a bit from Luc and me over the last year.

Warden Yar, Garbhan said silently.

From the boot treads, someone smaller followed the giant Light warden into the living area.

"Warden, I will guard my drawings, but I need you to fetch one of the Balance clerks to copy these to papyrus or parchment."

"Yar, stay here with the brother," Gina said. She had no problem countermanding a clergy member's order if she believed it was in their best interest. "I'll send Noko. It'll get her mind off the grotesque scene in here and the rewind." Gina crouched next to me. "Chief Justice?"

"I will need some help standing," I admitted. *Yanaba?*

I was bright enough to lay down before we started, she said with an irritated tone. *Sivan and Ming Wei are attending to me.*

Once Gina half-carried, half-guided me to the healer's wagon, Bly pressed a potion bottle to my hands while Devin checked my vitals. Noko shuffled nearby, no doubt to make sure I was all right before she faced Little Bear at the Temple.

"You all are worse than mother geese," I protested. However, I swigged Bly's concoction.

"That's because you refuse to use the sense the Twelve gave a dog," Devin snapped. "At least, your heartbeat is slowing. You're damn lucky it didn't seize."

"I'm fine. Besides, Justice Yanaba helped with the rewind." I immediately regretted my words. Both healers froze and scowled at me.

"Go on to Balance and check on her, Master Bly," Devin said. "Simi and I can deal with the mess here."

"Warden Noko, go with the master healer and then escort Clerk Leilani back down here," Gina said.

Noko audibly gulped. "Yes, Warden."

Part of me wished I could simply erase Noko's memory of the horrible scene inside the shop. She would no doubt relive what she saw during the rewind for the next week or so, too. That would add one more to the list of people at Balance having nightmares.

Bly grabbed a shoulder bag from the seat of the wagon. Together, she and Noko trotted down the side street toward the Temple District.

"How many times do we need to remind you not to put so much on Justice Yanaba, Anthea?" Devin murmured. His fingers rested against my neck once more to check my pulse.

Why had I asked Yanaba for help? She needed the rest.

Because I wanted to do only one rewind for the entire house. Normally, our gift for viewing the past is hindered by the need to anchor ourselves in three dimensions, which means we're limited by the walls of one room.

In Yanaba's effort to destroy the demons last spring, she'd let go of her body and anchored her spirit to the walls, streets, and buildings of the city. Shi Hua, Jeremy, and Brother Turtle from Child managed to disentangle Yanaba and place her spirit back into her body, but my junior justice was still linked to Orrin.

To the point she couldn't step outside the city walls or sail past the harbor entrance without nearly killing herself.

I couldn't worry about Yanaba at the moment. Instead, I needed to focus on the atrocities committed in the building before me. The creature had done its dismembering here, but did the actual deaths occur before it brought its victims to the shop? Balance only knew where it found these people. DiCook's confirmation of no reports of missing people didn't mean no one knew the victims were gone, only that their absence hadn't been officially recorded.

The thought of every possible lead to follow was adding to my post-rewind headache. And this very morning, I told myself I needed to carry more of the court load while Yanaba dealt with her babe. I couldn't imagine how I would handle everything without Elizabeth here, too.

"You're right," I replied equally softly to Devin. "I promise not to rely on her so much, but I fear putting too much on Chief Justice Elizabeth as well."

"She's doing much better than when she arrived here nearly six months ago." His eyebrow lifted as his fingers withdrew from my neck. I didn't need silent speech to know his unspoken question.

"Rebuilding and fortifying on Tuqan Island has begun, but it's a long way from being ready for regular habitation." I shook my head. "Crown Princess Chiara has thrown in her support for the project, but it's going to be expensive, and the queendom's treasury is already pushed to the limit."

"We didn't expect to lose an entire city," Devin remarked. "Or how it affected sea trade."

The hairs on the back of my neck rose despite being soaked in sweat. "No, but we didn't have much of a choice, and we paid a steeper price in the lives we lost."

"I wasn't blaming you, Anthea," he said gently.

"Why not?" I snapped. "Everyone else does." I jumped down from my seat on the edge of the wagon and marched back into the seamstress shop. The voices in the back of mind whispered that I'd done everything in my power, but they could give me more so something like Tandor would never happen again.

Shut up!

They went silent, except a hum of discussion amongst themselves. That noise I could ignore, just like when I ignored the wagons, horses, and people outside of Balance during a court session.

What I needed was a way to shut down the demons in my head for good, instead of dealing with murders of people who didn't matter.

Chapter 4

"What did you say?" Garbhan stared at me with an appalled expression as did Yar.

Heat rushed to my cheeks. I hadn't realized I'd spoken out loud, but I did realize how my words could be misconstrued.

"I apologize. I'm tired and hungry and nauseated . . ." I stared at the gruesome pile on the table, then pivoted to check the walls. Certain stains showed to my odd vision. Unfortunately, one of them was blood. However, something was off. Something I didn't notice until now. "There's no blood splatter other than on the floor around the table."

Yar nodded as he looked around the room. "And just where it dripped from the edge. Therefore, the victims were dead when the culprit brought them here."

"Can I let Master Devin in so he and Simi can collect the limbs?" I asked.

"Yes." Garbhan nodded sharply. "My warden and I will guard my drawings until your clerk arrives."

I and the representative from the Temple of Death were still at the Healer's Guild, observing the healers attempt to match limbs to each other, when Brother Garbhan and my clerk Leilani arrived along with Noko and Yar.

"I know you can't see my drawing of the creature the brother and Warden Noko witnessed, Chief Justice," Leilani said with a breathless rush. "But from the pattern of how it originally placed the limbs—"

"It definitely looks like it was trying to caste some kind of spell," Garbhan interrupted.

"Well, now the cat's out of the bag," Devin said a little louder than necessary. "That's what I was going to mention to you privately as well."

"You noticed the symbols?" I asked. "But the rats had already disrupted the positioning before you saw them."

"It's not any different than the rats running across parchment that was freshly written on with ink." Devin walked over and looked at Leilani's sketch. "It may still be readable. I'm glad someone else noticed the same patterns I observed." He grinned at Garbhan before returning to his work.

Sister Raven Claw eased closer to see Leilani's sketch. Nearly a century ago, the Healers Guild had split from the Temple of Death. Because of that rivalry, their home Temple in Standora insisted one of their clergy be present whenever I asked the Healers Guild to check an issue with a corpse in a suspected murder. But even as much as Raven Claw witnessed death in its many forms, she had issues keeping her stomach from rebelling with today's discovery. She still carried the scent of Master Healer Bly's peppermint concoction to soothe her digestive system.

"Dark magic?" Raven Claw asked.

Garbhan grunted in agreement.

"It used the limbs to form the ancient symbols for 'priest', 'war' and 'power'. If I may, Chief Justice?" Leilani held out her palm. I placed my right hand in her left. She folded her fingers around my index digit as if it were a stylus or pen, and she drew the symbols with my own finger so I could "see" them.

I frowned. "Is it declaring war on us? Or trying to force us to fight ourselves? And why invoke power?"

"If I may, Chief Justice?" Yar rumbled. He so rarely offered an opinion it took me by surprise for a moment.

I gestured for him to continue.

"Why didn't any of the neighbors report hearing anything last week?" The Light warden pointed at Leilani's picture of the creature. "Something of that size should have made a racket. Even if someone saw it and was afraid to venture from their dwelling or shop, they would have summoned the peacekeepers the next morning."

"Also, I checked the back door," Gina said. "It was locked. There's no scratches on the metal, so the lock wasn't picked. Or it could have been picked and relocked by a true expert. Given the creature's halfway appearance, maybe it was in human form before it entered the building. If so, and the fact it didn't enter the building until after the magistrate's sale, maybe no one thought twice about it, thinking it was the new owners."

I sighed and rubbed my temples. The headache from the rewind and the demon voices was growing worse.

"First of all, that's a lot of guesswork in so few sentences," I said. "The peacekeepers have learned to canvas neighborhoods properly. We'll put their findings with ours, and then deal with what we're missing."

"Chief Justice?" Bly called out.

"Did you find something?" I strode over to the main examination table, only for my stomach to start gurgling.

"You're not vomiting all over our work," Master Devin snapped and held up his right arm in an attempt to shield the remains.

"Unfortunately, those were hunger sounds," I said dryly.

The healers and their apprentices looked at me as if I were mad. The demon voices in the back of my mind jeered at me.

I ignored the voices and my heated cheeks. "What did you find?"

Bly held up a pair of forceps. The tip held a tiny chunk, but it was so covered in body fluids I couldn't tell what it was.

"It's a portion of talon caught in the femur of one of the victims." Bly grinned.

"We have a way to track the creature," I breathed. My stomach rumbled, and the voices in the back of my head cheered.

Now, why would the dead demons forming the grimoire I had hidden in my quarters be happy about tracking down an unknown creature?

Unless it was a corrupted human like a skinwalker.

Chapter 5

I had Garbhan take the lead on putting together a hunting party made up of clergy and wardens. If he wanted the experience and responsibility, I was more than happy to give it to him.

Once I finally settled in my office at Balance and drank my first pot of Jing black tea of the day while snacking on fruit, I summoned both Gina and Little Bear. From both of their expressions, Gina had warned my chief warden of my conversation with Brother Garbhan and Magistrate DiCook.

"May we simply address the reason we are here without the social niceties?" Little Bear grumbled.

"I find that odd considering you are usually the one lecturing me for not adhering to them." I stared at them both for a moment before I added in a more gentle tone, "Is it as bad as people are telling me?"

Gina snorted. "Actually, it's worse. He's not even leading dawn services anymore."

Little Bear shot her a warning look, but Gina raised her chin and said, "She needs to know as the seat of Balance. This isn't about their relationship."

Little Bear dropped into one of my visitor chairs. For him to breach decorum in that manner meant he was truly disturbed. "You need to go visit him, m'lady."

"And how do you propose I do that?" I waved in the direction of my bedchambers. "The tunnels are shut down, and we've disabled the Temple entrances to prevent anyone, human or demon, from entering the city again via those routes."

Except I made a new passage in my quarters to hide the demon grimoire I'd confiscated from my mother after I beheaded her. The voices in the back of my mind encouraged me to make the passage bigger. Then I could create a new passage into Light so I could visit Luc whenever I wanted. He owed me after all the time he spent with Claudia in his bed—

With a deep breath, I ignored the voices. I really needed to focus on getting Light functional again. Garbhan couldn't do everything, no matter how much he believed he could.

"You might want to try the front door," Gina said dryly.

"I did," I snapped. "He refused to see me."

Though honestly, Luc's head of household Istaqa was rather embarrassed when he asked me to leave the four times I traipsed across the boulevard to Light last month.

"Chief Warden Nicholas will hold Istaqa out of the way if you wish to try again," Little Bear said.

"Nicholas disobeying a direct order from the high brother?" I shook my head. "Another demon attack is far more likely than that."

"Not this time." Little Bear grimaced. "He showed me the empty wine skins and bottles. He's worried. Shi Hua is bedridden. Jeremy's frightened for her and still having nightmares from the Battle of Tandor despite aid from Child. Garbhan is the only functional Light priest we have at the moment."

"And it's probably not a coincidence this creature is killing humans when we are low on Light capable clergy," Gina added.

"So you are expecting me to fix the high brother? He needs someone from Child, not me." If Luc blamed me for my mother killing his child, so be it. Our relationship was illegal prior to the new edict anyway.

Besides, the bitch tried to abort me. She was the reason I couldn't give Luc a child anyway.

I blinked to clear the extra moisture from my eyes.

Gina placed her hands on the back of the other visitor chair. "I understand why the two of you are uncomfortable around each other. But you're also taking your uncomfortableness out on Sister Shi Hua. You haven't even tried to visit her in the last two months. She can't come here, and she needs all the support she can get."

"The ambassador and his concubine have been—"

"But Yin Li can't be there all the time, and—" Gina shot a glance at Little Bear who gave her a slight nod.

She sucked a deep breath and continued, "Justice Yanaba is restricted to Balance until she delivers."

I jerked to my feet. "Is she all right? Her baby's not in danger, is she?"

"Calm down, m'lady." Little Bear gestured for me to resume my seat. "She's quite well, and so is the babe. This is a precautionary measure."

"This is because I asked for her help this morning, isn't it?" I slammed my fist onto the top of my desk. "Devin was furious she helped me with the rewind spell, and this is his revenge."

"No, m'lady. This has nothing to do with the Healers Guild, though Master Healer Bly was not happy Yanaba exerted herself this morning." Little Bear sighed. "After the incident with Sister Claudia, the chief wardens met concerning protection of the remaining three Light pregnancies."

"Three?" I feigned innocence.

"Nice try." Sarcasm laced Gina's words. "It's only a matter of time before Sister Cedar Grove starts showing. And after your rather bold announcement of Lady Katarina's condition, we all know you can see a pregnancy before the mother's even aware."

I grimaced. My congratulations had put a crimp in the duke and his wife's relationship since she hadn't told him prior to my comment. It hadn't been one of my finer moments in manners and etiquette.

After clearing my throat, I asked. "So what precautions have you wardens put in place?"

"We've put together plans for getting all three priestesses out of the Temples if there's another attempt on their lives. And it's on a need to know basis," he added sternly.

"But Yanaba is my responsibility," I protested.

Gina chuckled. "High Brother Xander said the same thing. Neither of you are asking the young justice's opinion."

I swore under my breath. "This is about the price on my head."

"We can't give the Assassins Guild two easy targets in Balance," Little Bear said, confirming my fears.

"Like having Yanaba preside in court," I murmured. "She's going to think I'm punishing her." Maybe she deserved to be punished. She made no secret the Reverend Mother sent her here to spy on me, and if necessary, replace me.

I rubbed at the ache in my temples. I was obviously too tired if I were allowing petty thoughts like that to cloud my mind. Except the voices confirmed that I was right to feel the way I did.

My stomach rumbled. I had broken my fast far earlier than normal this morning, and the small bowl of fruit wasn't enough. Maybe the ache in my head would go away with a decent meal. It was only logical to take advantage of Light's hospitality and their cook's excellent cuisine during the midday meal.

"I'll visit with Sister Shi Hua now, and attempt—" At my wardens' pleased expressions, I held up my right palm. "—attempt to speak with the high brother. I make no guarantees."

"Even an attempt would soothe Nicholas's concerns," Gina murmured.

"I don't think I will miss your nagging when you leave with Chief Justice Elizabeth," I snapped.

Gina merely grinned. "I'll miss everyone here as well, m'lady."

Wardens Daniel and Ahiga accompanied me to the Temple of Light, even though it was quite literally across the street from the Temple of Balance. Ever since the Assassins Guild's attempt to slit my throat on the steps of Light, my wardens wouldn't let me travel outside our Temple walls without them.

Since the renewed demon attacks, I could barely go to the privy without one of them either.

The Light warden guarding the main doors inclined his head to me and my escort. He didn't bar me from entering the Temple itself.

My escort and I strode into the sanctuary. Except for the crisp scent of incense from the dawn services and the orderly benches, it was empty. Not even one of the private consultation rooms were in use. The eternal flame at the base of the statue of Light glowed blindingly white, and I squinted.

One of the attendants entered the sanctuary and bowed to me. No doubt Istaqa sent his staff member out to meet me because the Light head of household was tired of dealing with my demands.

"I beg forgiveness, Lady Justice, but the high brother—" he began.

"I'm here for a social visit with Sister Shi Hua," I said. "I regret I have been remiss in allowing my duties to interfere with our friendship." My stomach rumbled again.

"She would be most pleased if you would join her for the noon meal." The attendant bowed to me again before leading the way to Shi Hua's quarters. It wasn't like I didn't know where they were, but caution reinforced the Temple protocols.

Warden Mateqai stood at attention beside the priestess's door. He inclined his head and knocked on the lacquered wood.

"Yes?" Shi Hua called out.

Mateqai opened the door a crack and peered inside. "The chief justice is here to see you, m'lady."

"Anthea! Come in!"

Mateqai turned to face me with a barely suppressed grin. "Sister Shi Hua will see you now, Lady Justice."

I entered the priestess's bed chambers. The tingle of light balls caressed my skin. Shi Hua herself was propped on a multitude of pillows on her bed to the extent she looked like a child's doll. Her hair was loose and cascaded over her shoulders. Instead of a uniform tunic and leggings, she wore a cotton shift that accommodated her growing belly. Her bright smile lifted my own spirits.

"How are you doing?" I crossed to the bed and hugged her.

"I'll be better," she said. I released her and sat down in the chair next to her bed. She glared at Mateqai. "Once all the nosey wardens close my door."

He promptly obeyed her, and her wards sprung up in the room the instant the door shut and latched.

I pushed back my hood and cocked my head. "Is that really necessary?"

She groaned, leaned her head back against the pillows, and closed her eyes. "You have no idea, Anthea. I never dreamed kindness could be used as a torture device. They treat me like a total invalid."

"They're concerned about your welfare and the babe's," I murmured.

She opened her eyes and glared at me. "If you're going to nag me, too—"

"This is a social visit." I waved in the direction of the door. "But aren't you worrying your wardens unnecessarily?"

Shi Hua sniffed with contempt. "You think I haven't had to do this before? The bedrest is bad enough, but the constant harping of every man here!" She shook her head. "They act like this is the first baby ever conceived!"

"Well, it is the first pregnancy for any clergy of the Orrin Temple of Light," I retorted.

We both laughed long and loud.

Shi Hua wiped her eyes. "Thank you. I needed that. I'm assuming Garbhan shared our worries with you."

I sighed. "The magistrate volunteered his two coppers before Garbhan did. However, I am remiss in not visiting you over the last several weeks."

"*Pfft.*" She waved her hand dismissively. "You've had your own issues to deal with."

"That's no excuse."

"Anthea, your mother consorted in demon magic, and you beheaded her." Shi Hua reached over and took my left hand in her right. "Even for children raised in the Temples like us, that affects your spirit. If I was forced to do the same to my aunt or cousin in order to protect my child—" She shuddered and rubbed her swollen belly.

"The difference is you care about your birth family," I muttered.

She shook her head. "I don't need a truthspell to see you're lying, Anthea."

The voices murmured that they could take my pain away. For an instant, I wanted to believe them. I needed to change the subject before my emotions overtook me.

"If it's any consolation, Yanaba is restricted to Balance as well."

Shi Hua squeezed my hand. "Is that why you look exhausted?"

"I am not exhausted," I snapped.

"Mm-hmmm." She gave me a wry grin. "Why does the skin under your eyes look like you applied a thick layer of kohl?"

"All right." I stuck out my tongue at her, and she laughed. "I didn't sleep well last night, and I finish a rewind not long ago. I'd really love to take a nap, but—"

"You'll just have more nightmares," she said softly.

"Yes, but—"

Shi Hua's warding spell muffled the knocking on her bedchamber door, but I definitely recognized the masculine roar of anger.

"Now, what's got his small clothes in a wad?" I couldn't help the thick layer of sarcasm in my words.

"Garbhan and the wardens won't tattle on me, but Jeremy or Istaqa would," she said sourly. "They all get angry if I ward my room for a little privacy."

"I bet a silver on Istaqa tattling." I grinned at her.

"I want a cocoa cinnamon pastry from the Meca place on Bakers Street if it's Jeremy." Shi Hua's expression lit up.

More pounding was followed by another roar of fury. There was a time when it would take far more than someone warding their bedchamber to anger Luc.

"Let me guess," I said as I rose from the chair. "Istaqa has you on what he considers an appropriate diet for the child."

Shi Hua groaned. "And the high brother threatened to lash Mateqai if he snuck anymore pastries into the Temple for me."

That statement blew off the lid of my own rage. Mateqai would never do anything to harm Shi Hua or her baby. As long as he didn't tell anyone the treat was for Shi Hua, it would be perfectly safe. And I couldn't see him be anything but protective. Twelve blast it, he had been acting as her taster since the Assassins Guild tried to poison me.

At my nod, Shi Hua dropped her wards, and I yanked the door open. Sure enough, a guilty looking Jeremy stood behind his high brother. And Luc's skin glowed a brilliant pink behind his raised fist.

"What in Balance are you barking about?" I shouted. "Not every priestess wants to share every intimate detail of her body with a bunch of fishwives like you lot!"

Luc jerked back from the door and lowered his fist. The foul mix of unwashed body and alcohol fumes emanating from him made my eyes water. But even with my odd vision blurred by burning tears, I could see his blue hair stood at wild angles and blue stubble covered the lower half of his face. In the eleven years I'd known him, the only time he'd gone unshaven was when a demon army laid siege to Tandor, and the city's water supply had been cut off.

Behind him, both his wardens and mine tensed. However, Nicholas had a slightly smug look on his bearded visage.

"I gave her a direct order not to ward her room from the wardens," Luc growled. "If a demon gets in disguised as—"

"Me?" I poked him in the chest. "The entire city knows you're furious with me over the death of your child, but you're taking it out on everyone else in this damn Temple. Enough is enough! Get a bath and sober up, or I will call a convocation on charges of dereliction of duty, High Brother." I slurred his title into an insult.

"How dare you," he breathed. His color flared to a deeper pink. "How dare you!"

"What are you going to do about it?" I stepped closer despite his awful smell until we were nose to nose. "Challenge me to a duel right at this moment?"

The muscle along his right jaw trembled. I didn't need to touch his mind to know he was embarrassed I'd backed him into a trap. He was in no condition to fight me, even if he still had his left foot. He didn't have any weapons on him. And he was barely upright on his crutches as it was.

"Are you going to draw steel on the chief justice, High Brother?" Nicholas asked. Given the circumstances, doing so would be a good way for Luc to lose his head.

Instead of answering either me or Nicholas, Luc turned and staggered back down the hallway. Mateqai and the new Light warden, whose name I couldn't remember for the life of me at the moment, let him pass.

I glared at Luc's second. "Jeremy, might I suggest that if you ever hope to share the sister's bed again that you stop tattling on her? The high brother's order against warding her own damn room is ridiculous, and you know it. Do we really want to cause a diplomatic incident with Jing?"

"No, m'lady." The younger priest's face glowed a brilliant crimson. Whether at my tongue-lashing or the fear he'd irreparably damaged his relationship with Shi Hua was up for debate.

I turned to Nicholas. "Chief Warden, please do everyone a favor."

"Of course, Lady Justice," he replied.

"When the high brother passes out, drop him into his bathing pool." I shook my head. "Before his stench chokes all of you to death."

Chapter 6

Despite the, well, I couldn't call it a fight with Luc, I had a pleasant meal with Shi Hua. In my own wallowing, I'd forgotten how much I enjoyed the young priestess's company.

"May I ask a favor?"

"If I can," she said with a smile.

"Do you think Ambassador Quan or his concubine would object if Nathan attends the language and martial arts lessons with Ming Wei?"

From her expression, she understood why I was couching my words in such delicate terms. We didn't have the warding to protect us. Only a few people knew her aunt was really the Jing ambassador's bodyguard. Even fewer knew Ambassador Quan was the Jing emperor's half-brother. And only three people outside of Shi Hua's bedchamber knew Mistress Yin Li was actually a Love priestess.

Better yet, if Shi Hua needed to get a message to me without using silent speech, she could employ my squire.

The priestess smiled and nodded. "I will ask, but I don't believe they will object. And please visit me since Yanaba can no longer come over. I need women to talk to."

I could understand her feelings. Jing's Temple of Light had all genders as part of their membership. Issura insisted on men only, not just clergy, but wardens and attendants as well. It had been a major adjustment for the personnel here when Shi Hua was transferred to Orrin's

44

Temple of Light. The Issuran standard seemed even more ridiculous when we were facing more demon invasions, and we needed every person with Light talent we could find.

"I will," I promised.

I left her quarters with my two wardens in tow. No one bothered to escort us through the Temple, though Mateqai had a pleased expression on his face as we passed him, which I was sure stemmed from me standing up for his charge.

When we entered the sanctuary again, Garbhan and Yar waited along with Sisquoc from the Wildling Temple, two priests from Conflict, and more surprisingly, two priests from Father. Only Sisquoc didn't have a warden accompanying him.

"Where is your warden, Brother?" I narrowed my eyes, but the huge Wildling didn't flinch from my red gaze.

"I don't need one." Sisquoc jutted out his chin as if daring me to argue with him.

I really couldn't argue his point. His second form was a mountain panther. I'd seen him in action against renegades, skinwalkers, and demons. No, he didn't really need a warden.

Instead, I said, "Don't expect me to watch your back."

"It's not my back my high brother is concerned about, but yours." He managed not to flash a cheeky grin, but his humor rolled over my mental shields. It was as warm and soft as his fur.

"We all need to be careful," Garbhan interjected.

"You showed everyone Leilani's drawings?" I asked. All the men murmured their acknowledgement of having seen the description.

"Did any of you recognize it?" I looked at each of their faces, but they all shook their heads.

"We did confer with the Temple of Knowledge," Garbhan said. "Not even High Sister Mariana had heard of anything like this creature. She assured me she would assign someone to research the matter."

I bit my tongue to keep from giving my opinion of who Mariana would assign to the task, much less whether they would find any worthwhile information. There was so much the Temple of Knowledge hadn't recorded because they assumed such common lore wouldn't be forgotten. Then there was the fact that Mariana considered requests from the other Temples to be of less of a priority than her own tasks. She didn't do so out of spite, but simply because she didn't understand their importance.

On the other hand, I didn't know why I was worried about Mariana's feelings. She had voted to condemn me to Orrin's Balance seat last year after I killed Samael DiRoy, the queen's cousin, in order to banish the demons he had summoned.

In fact, no one in Orrin cared about the sacrifices I'd made to protect them. No, they blamed the Red Justice for all their troubles instead of—

"Chief Justice?" Garbhan said loudly.

All of the priests and wardens stared at me.

"I beg your pardon, Brother?"

"I asked if you were ready to perform the tracking spell." His brows formed a blue "V". He must have been trying to get my attention for longer than I realized.

"It would be best of one of the others assists you," I said. "The rewind this morning took more out of me than I realized."

"Of course, Chief Justice." He inclined his head.

"I'll assist you, Brother," one of the Conflict priests murmured.

Together, they knelt before the eternal flame. A bowl with a few shavings of the creature's cleaned talon sat between them. As Garbhan said, we often had far less to work with in a tracking spell, and not using all of it at one time would give us a second opportunity.

Just in case.

It was odd not to see one of the other three Light clergy with him though. Things were simply changing too fast. And we were losing Light talents faster than we could breed them. Thanks to my mother I couldn't do my share. If Luc couldn't pull himself out of his well of grief, or Twelve forbid, we lost Shi Hua due to her delivery . . .

The two men chanted, but the Conflict priest's voice was discordant compared to the rhythms of Light. Their magic prickled along my skin, the harsh buzz of the warrior a counterpoint to the insistent tickle of truth. Garbhan lit a reed from the eternal flame and set the contents of the bowl on fire. The energies mixed and formed an invisible ribbon that arrowed for the open door of the Temple of Light.

Diamond-sharp blackness surrounded the ribbon and exploded with the force of a bag of Jing flash powder. The cold rush of power knocked me backward. I slammed into a worshippers' bench and flipped over it. The hilts of my knives dug into my hip bones, my scabbard into my spine and ribs, as I tumbled across the floor.

When I came to a rest, I wondered what it would cost to overlay Balance's marble floor with wooden planks. I didn't hurt half as bad as I did after being thrown into stone, though my head pounded.

It wasn't just my head. The Temple bells rang the alert for demons.

Ahiga, one of my own wardens, knelt next to me. "Lady Justice?"

"I'm still alive." I grabbed the hand he offered to assist me in sitting upright. "What about Garbhan?"

I looked around us. The wardens were all upright. It was only the clergy on the floor.

This wasn't a normal trap spell. A metallic taste filled my mouth. Demon magic.

Except it didn't feel as alien as it had before.

The priest who had been assisting Garbhan sat up with some aid from his warden. "What in Conflict's Hammer happened?"

"Chief Justice!" Yar's alarm prickled painfully against my psyche. He knelt next to Garbhan who wasn't moving.

"Is he alive?" I asked.

At the same moment, Brother Jeremy rushed into the room along with a handful of Light wardens. "What happened?"

"A tracking spell gone wrong," Sisquoc spat. A fine layer of blue fur covered him. My other warden Daniel assisted the Wildling as he tamed his second form.

"He's not breathing!"

Ahiga helped me to my feet, and I stumbled nearer to the prone Garbhan. Yar pinched the priest's nose shut and breathed into his mouth. Another Light warden knelt on Garbhan's left side and performed chest compressions.

I could only stare at the scene, though Jeremy shouted orders and one of their squires raced back to the stables to fetch a healer. Another Light talent was dying, and it was my fault.

Chapter 7

I ignored Luc as he hobbled into the sanctuary and stood next to me on his crutches. His hair had a greenish tint, his beard was gone, and he smelled of imported Aleppo soap. Since he said nothing to me, I focused my prayers to the Twelve on Brother Garbhan's survival.

The tolling of the demon alarm bells died while Yar and the other Light warden continued their administrations, breathing and pumping the priest's heart for him. Finally, Garbhan gasped and started choking.

"Roll him over," Yar barked. Together, the two wardens turned the young man over to his left side. Garbhan vomited a small bit of bile, but his stomach was still empty from the scene at the seamstress shop this morning.

"Out of the way! Out of the way!" Master Healer Devin pushed past the observers to get to Garbhan's side. Two journeymen followed him. The wardens moved aside now that Garbhan was breathing on his own.

"What in the Twelve happened?" Devin glared at me while his journeymen healers checked Garbhan's breathing and heartbeat. "We had both Justice Yanaba and Sister Shi Hua screaming in our minds there was an attack at Light right as the Temple bells started pealing the demon alert."

"A bit of demon magic was on the talon Master Bly found." I started shaking my head, but I quickly discovered that was a poor idea. "None of us detected it before Brother Garbhan and—" I looked around for the Conflict priest.

"Brother Pimu," the young priest offered. High Brother Han was standing next to him. In fact, the sanctuary of Light was filled with clergy and wardens from all the Temples. Pimu looked up at Han. "I can attest to the Chief Justice's statement. I'm grateful Brother Garbhan only used a few shavings. I fear the hidden spell would have killed everyone in the sanctuary if we'd used more."

"Why was Pimu assisting Garbhan?" Luc snapped at me.

"Because I'm having to train your people as well as mine!" I wanted to slap him. No, I wanted to stab him. Right in the heart like he'd done to me by laying with Claudia. I reached for my dagger.

"That's enough!" High Mother Leocadia barked as she stepped between us. "From both of you!" She turned to the crowd. "The entertainment is over. High Brother Han, if you would coordinate with the magistrate and the other Temples? The suspect in the seamstress shop murders could still be within the city."

Han nodded. "Extra patrols would be an excellent idea, High Mother."

Devin let out a deep sigh. "If we could get some assistance loading Brother Garbhan in our wagon—"

"You can take him to his quarters for healing," Luc snapped.

"I need some peace and quiet, and I'm not getting any here." Devin rose and glared at Luc for a long moment before he turned to the Conflict contingent standing nearby. "You, too, Brother Pimu. I want to know why you didn't receive the same damage as Brother Garbhan."

"All of the clergy went down when the tracking spell set off whatever demon magic was in the talon shavings," Ahiga said.

"Be quiet." I whirled to scowl at him.

"Warden Ahiga speaks truly," Yar said. "They all suffered the effects of the demon magic. Almost as if a giant winter storm swept through the Temple and felled them like trees."

Devin gave a long, exasperated sigh. "Wardens, would you please collect your clergy who were present for the tracking spell?"

"Traitor," I hissed to Ahiga. His visage remained as stony as Little Bear's when he was irritated with something I'd done.

"And, Wardens." High Mother Leocadia's smile would have had High Bother Jax of Wildling hiding his tail between his legs. "If your charges give you any trouble, come get me."

The Healers Guild staff cleaned the Patient House with a religious zeal no Temple could match. But all the lemon oil and lye soap in the world could not cover the odor of illness and death that permeated the building.

It meant I'd need to take another bath when I returned to Balance. I swallowed my fury as Master Bly and Chief Healer Aaron had me strip off my clothing. They examined every inch of me, internally as well as externally. It wasn't the lack of clothing that bothered me. It was the lack of weapons. I wanted to strike at something, anything to release the anger that this creature had tricked us.

When I said as much, Bly shrugged. "Master Devin warned us you were about to draw on High Brother Luc."

"Is everyone around here a snitch?" I grumbled.

"When it comes to keeping the citizens of Orrin healthy, then yes," Aaron replied. "Your rage could be a symptom of the demon spell imbedded in the talon."

"Pimu was part of the tracking spell that released the demon magic, not me," I complained.

"But the renegades would only consider him collateral damage," Bly said. "You and everyone from Light are the ones with prices on their heads."

I sighed. As much as I hated to admit it, the healers were right. Light talent could do the most damage to a demon without in turn causing harm to humans. With my peculiar sight, I could see demons regardless of their shapeshifting or their glamours. The only time I couldn't see their true nature was when they wore a human skin.

Perhaps the creature Garbhan and Noko witnessed was a variant of a skinwalker. Or the demons used the skin of a creature from their own plane to disguise themselves.

No, that didn't make sense. All the creatures of this world looked the same to me, a riot of colors. It made more sense that anything from the demons' plane would be the same black they were. But there could be other planes of existence they had already conquered. Other creatures. And a priest nearly died trying to learn the truth.

"How is Garbhan?" I asked softly.

"He's awake, and Devin repaired as much of the damage to the boy's heart and lungs as he could," Aaron murmured. Well, that explained the waves of warmth in my chest. The chief healer was checking my own organs for injury.

"Long term prognosis?" I asked.

The warmth receded, and Master Aaron looked me in the eye. "Better than your squire, m'lady, but worse than Brother Pimu."

Pain swept through me at the reminder of the harm to Nathan. The Assassins Guild had poisoned the healers' sweet almond oil supply. The exposed adults like me had survived, but the dosage had caused a great deal of damage to my squire's heart. He couldn't run and play for as long as a normal child because his little heart simply couldn't keep up. It was a good part of the reason he and Ming Wei had become close. They drew strength from each other despite their physical limitations.

We could help you fix the children, the demon voices whispered. *We can help you make them strong again.*

"You lie," I spat.

"No, I am not, Chief Justice." Master Aaron stepped back stiffly, his color a brighter orange than usual.

Once again, I'd been caught responding to that damn grimoire. I needed to be more careful. If anyone found out I still had that book of demon magic, I could lose my head.

Strike that. I *would* lose my head.

I cleared my throat. "I apologize, Master Aaron. That comment was not aimed at you."

"If you are talking to yourself that much, perhaps you should speak to someone at the Temple of Child," Bly suggested.

"Me?" I scoffed. "What about the drunken mess that is the high brother of Light?"

"We are discussing your health, both mental and physical, Chief Justice," Aaron replied gruffly. "Not his."

I groaned. "None of this would be happening if the Reverend Mother of Balance had done her job and beheaded . . . Gerd." I had to choke out my mother's name.

You did the right thing, the voices whispered. *She was cruel and a fool. You are so much better than she was.*

I rubbed my temples wishing there was a way to make the dead demons be quiet.

Bly frowned at me. "Does your head pain you, Chief Justice?" She immediately began double-checking my scalp.

I considered lying, but there was no reason to deny my other problems. In fact, they provided excellent excuses. "Yes, but it started long before the tracking spell. I haven't been sleeping well the last couple of months."

"Since Gerd kidnapped and stabbed Sister Claudia?" Aaron's voice had a wee bit of sympathy.

"That along with today's rewind." I played along and let my shoulders sag. "I've had nightmares nearly every night. If I could get one good night's rest . . ."

Bly stepped back and glanced at Aaron. "One drop of soma tears in a cup of milk before you retire for the night. One time only. If you don't sleep tonight, come back here tomorrow."

"You have something stronger than soma tears?" I asked with a little too much hope in my voice.

"No," she said sternly. "I'll have you spend the night with Master Una."

"I do not need a dreamwalker," I snapped. "I know the cause of my nightmares."

"The alternative is going to the Temple of Child," she said mildly.

I was stuck, and I knew it. I exhaled heavily. "All right, you win."

Bly simply nodded at my acquiescence, but Aaron gave me a strange look. A look I couldn't decipher. Part of me wanted to link with him to find out what he was thinking, but maybe it would be best I didn't know. Nor could I take the chance he would Hear my little problems.

"And before you think of crossing me—" Bly folded her arms over her chest. "—I'll send a messenger to Sivan with my prescription."

"Now, that's just playing dirty, Master Healer." I grinned at her.

"And I've learned how to deal with recalcitrant patients by observing how Masters Aaron and Devin deal with you," she retorted.

They finally allowed me to dress after finding only the impact bruises from being tossed across Light's sanctuary by the demon magic. It was interesting how the physical effects of the hidden spell on the claw shavings only affected those of us in the sanctuary with talent.

Or did it? I knew neither Ahiga nor Daniel had any passive talent. I would have to check into the other wardens who were present.

Bly escorted me to the foyer of the Patient House where my wardens waited for me. I turned to her. "Thank you for your assistance today, Master Healer. I'm sorry for being difficult."

A wry grin appeared on her face. "Maybe we should do a second check on your brain. I mean, really? Chief Justice Anthea apologizing?"

The voices urged me to punish her for the insult. I opted with saying, "Good noontide, Master Healer."

I flipped up my hood and followed Daniel out into the summer heat. Temple bells started tolling, and I paused, my muscles tense, but they rang Second Afternoon. Was it that late in the day already?

"I'm afraid so, Chief Justice," Ahiga murmured.

"Did I say that out loud?"

"No, m'lady," Daniel replied. "You used silent speech."

My cheeks heated in a way that had nothing to do with the afternoon sun. I hadn't slipped like that since my early years as a novice. "I'm sorry. I hope Master Bly's advice works. My entire staff doesn't need to hear my every random thought."

"The effect of the hidden spell effected all of the clergy," Ahiga commented. "We're simply glad you were not more severely injured. Some rest and some tea is what you truly need."

No, sleep was what I truly needed. I just prayed I would actually get some tonight.

The three of us remained silent as we walked back to Balance. I wasn't sure how I would manage the rest of this investigation without someone from Light. I'd put the last mentally and physically fit priest at the Temple in harm's way. Maybe I should consult with High Brother Jax of Wildling and High Brother Talbert of Thief about casting the tracking spell.

Or maybe ask Sister Claudia for assistance. She had a measure of Light talent. If I accidentally got her killed, I wouldn't think about her in bed with Luc anymore.

Sivan waited for us at the main doors of Balance. Rather, she waited for me.

"You have a guest in your office, Chief Justice."

I sighed again. I'd been doing that a lot lately. Luc hadn't been around for the last two months to nag me about the habit.

"What now?"

"High Sister Mya chose not to enlighten me." Sivan had an odd expression on her face. "She said the matter was between the two of you."

I stalked toward my office. Whatever game Mya played at, I was definitely not in the mood.

<h1 align="center">*Chapter 8*</h1>

High Sister Mya of Child sat in one of the visitor chairs and calmly sipped my expensive Jing black tea from a cup when I entered my office.

"Good noontide, Chief Justice." She smiled politely.

"It's closer to eventide," I said. "We did not have an appointment to meet today."

"No, we did not. I was here for Squire Ming Wei's session. It's much easier on her knowing you and Justice Yanaba are nearby." She set the cup aside. "She asked me to speak with you. As did High Brother Luc."

I flipped back my hood and narrowed my eyes. "I have nothing to say about the latter."

"I suspected that would be your response." She cocked her head. "But surely we can discuss Justice Yanaba's squire. You are still the Chief Justice of Orrin, the seat of Balance, are you not?"

Instead of answering her, I asked, "Where's Talbert to protect you from the agony of my anger and generally disagreeable attitude?"

She ignored my jibe. "Anthea, either Ming Wei has a touch of talent, or you are projecting."

"I hear." I picked up a clean sheet of papyrus. "You need my authorization to test her." I began stamping the official request.

"Her dreams have changed," Mya continued. "She describes a newborn soaked in blood, and she sees herself taking Gerd's head."

I paused, my hand tight about the handle of the stamp, but I couldn't

57

look directly at Mya. "I'll ward my quarters when I retire for the night. That should prevent the girl from seeing my dreams."

"Most likely." Mya picked up her cup and took another sip. "It doesn't address the fact you are still having nightmares about Gerd abducting you, Luc, and Claudia."

My head rose, and I glared at her. "Is that what you call it?" I sneered. "Mere abduction?"

"You beheaded your birth mother to save the city," Mya said gently. "And she in turn murdered your lover's child. I haven't met anyone who wouldn't have nightmares over such a situation."

"Thank you for your observation." Sarcasm ran thick in my voice. I wanted to kick her out of my Temple, but that would only make her look more closely at me. As if I had something to hide.

Which I did.

"You did something right." She retained that sickly sweet smile.

"Oh, and what is that?"

"In protecting Sister Shi Hua, you got High Brother Luc to come see me this afternoon."

"Isn't that wonderful?" I snarled before I resumed angrily stamping the request to have Ming Wei tested. I prayed to the Twelve for the child's sake she didn't have any talent. She'd been through enough in her short life.

"You're not the only one who feels guilty about what Gerd did to Claudia."

I set aside my stamps. "Is that what you think I feel? Guilt?"

"Isn't it?" One slim blue eyebrow rose on her forehead.

"No, I am furious." I slapped my right palm on the top of my desk. "My own Reverend Mother should have tried Gerd as soon as she arrived back in Standora. Instead, she let Gerd live for months. Those idiotic decisions gave Gerd a chance to escape and to—" I snapped my mouth shut before I said anything about the grimoire.

For once, the damn voices went silent, as if they were holding their breath, waiting to hear what I would say. Maybe not holding their breath exactly. They were dead, their own skins used to create the grimoire.

Yanaba had sworn up and down the Reverend Mother had destroyed the damned tome before the assembled justices when she returned to the home Temple in Standora. But the grimoire hidden in my bedchambers was the same one Gerd had planned to sell to the renegades. The same one I confiscated and turned over to the Reverend Mother.

"And to what, Anthea?" Mya asked gently.

I swallowed hard. "If Gerd couldn't rule Orrin, she planned to destroy it." I leaned my elbows on the surface of my desk. "She had started to turn into a skinwalker because she was using demon magic. I thought I'd given up on her, but I . . ." Hot tears stung my eyes and threatened to fall. I turned away from Mya and blinked several times to clear the extra liquid.

"There's nothing wrong with wishing you had your mother back." Mya laid her hands over mine. "Unfortunately, you had to do your duty, else she would have killed thousands of innocents."

"I know that." I jerked my hands away from Mya's touch. "But if the Reverend Mother didn't have the fortitude to do her own duty, she should have let me behead her last winter."

"Very well," Mya murmured. "I'll let that subject go for now. However, I am here if you need to talk—"

"I don't," I snapped.

"—or if you wish a different member of my Temple, that can be arranged, too," Mya finished as if I'd said nothing. "May I ask a different question?"

"That depends." I leaned back in my chair.

"What exactly did you say to High Brother Luc this morning to get him to come see me?" This time, a mischievous grin filled her face.

I frowned. "He didn't tell you?"

"No." She sipped her tea. "And his people are loyal to a fault. I was hoping you could give me some insight before my next session with him."

I sighed. "He has refused to see me since the healers . . . told us the babe couldn't be saved. He's been rather vile with everyone. Staff, clergy, and wardens alike. I let his attitude affect my friendship with Sister Shi Hua." I started to shake my head, only for the ache to remind me it wasn't a good idea. "So I made a point of visiting her. He was a mess. Unwashed for at least a week from the smell. Obviously drunk. And he shouted at the sister for merely wanting some privacy for women talk."

Mya gestured for me to continue as she poured herself some more tea. Maybe I was letting Luc's poor behavior rub off on me. As the hostess, I should have made sure her cup was filled.

"I told him if he didn't take a bath and sober up, I would call a convocation on him for dereliction of duty."

Tea sprayed from Mya's mouth, and she started coughing. She quickly set down her cup and covered her mouth with her sleeve until the fit subsided. "I'm sorry for that."

"That I was forced to threaten him, or for you finding it so shocking you choked on your tea?"

"Both," she said. "What happened next?"

"Oh, the tale gets better." I smirked. "When he yelled at me for daring to question him, I asked him if he was challenging me to a duel."

Mya's eyes widened. "He didn't, did he?"

"I think his chief warden bluntly asking him if he planned to draw steel on me sobered him more than a cold bath." I ran my fingers across Ming Wei's request for testing. "Our relationship may be irreparable, but I won't tolerate him taking his anger with me out on his people."

"Thank you for you time, Chief Justice." Mya stood and brushed at the damp spots on her robes. "I know you're busy with your investigation."

"The woman who bought Barbora's shop—" I began as I rose and handed the testing request for Ming Wei to Mya.

Mya smiled again. "Mistress Jaci's already made arrangements for her family to receive care. Her older sister is from Tandor, and she and her daughter have already been coming to my Temple."

"What about the rest of the refugees?" I asked.

"Most of them have come." Mya chuckled. "Between the evacuation and the summer riot, they realize they need someone to talk to in order to deal with their losses."

"Your Temple has been almost as busy as mine," I murmured.

"In some ways, busier." Mya shrugged. "We each have our role to play, Anthea. I don't envy yours. I like being able to help people."

And my role was to figure out what in Balance ate those people in Barbora's shop, and what exactly it planned to do with the limbs it left behind.

Chapter 9

I ate my evening meal at my desk as I tried to catch up on my own court's paperwork and the dispatches from the capital. Except my thoughts kept going to the tracking spell gone wrong.

Luc had stood beside me as first the wardens, then the healers, tended to Garbhan. But once the danger passed, he left the sanctuary without saying much to me or anyone else. He couldn't keep dumping everything on Jeremy.

Anymore than I could keep doing the same to Yanaba.

At the knock on my office door, I half-expected Elizabeth wanting to review the day's cases. She'd been chief justice of Tandor in her own right, and she was careful to acquiesce to my authority here in Orrin.

Except for the time she and Yanaba plotted against you and threatened to oust you as chief justice for daring to pursue your mother, the voices reminded me.

The hard part was I couldn't be sure whether it was the demons talking or my own petty internal monologue.

Whoever was in the corridor knocked again. I reached out with my mind. Little Bear stood outside along with High Mother Leocadia and her own warden.

"Enter," I called out.

The door swung open and Little Bear stepped inside. "High Mother Leocadia requests to speak with you, Chief Justice."

I pushed aside the dispatch I'd been reading. "Send her in. Could you have Sivan bring in another pot of tea for us?"

Little Bear nodded. "She's already working on it." He picked up the tray on my desk and left.

Leocadia strode into my office. Her warden started to enter, and the high mother essentially shut the door in the woman's face. The Temple of Mother didn't have a requirement that all of their wardens be women, but Leocadia replaced Mother's entire complement of wardens when she was assigned to the seat in Orrin. Her theory was the wardens who were not directly involved in her predecessor Bianca's schemes had failed in their duty to notice or report the illegal activities.

For her first month in the city, she thought about how to replace me, too, thanks to High Father Jerrod whispering in her ear. She changed her opinion after tagging along on my investigation into Claudia's abduction.

"To what do I owe the pleasure, High Mother?" I gesture for her to take a seat.

"I'm here about the incident with Brother Garbhan this afternoon," she said crisply as she sat in the closest visitor chair.

I tensed at the subject. "I apologize for arguing with the High Brother of Light. As I told everyone else, I didn't sleep well last night—"

"Tut-tut." She waved to dismiss my excuse. "That wasn't where I was going, but it was best you weren't part of the spell casting if you weren't fully rested. Things could have ended much worse otherwise."

"Then what exactly are you suggesting?" I said stiffly.

"That I assist you in casting the tracking spell." She had an air of being pleased with herself.

"But the Temple of Mother—"

"Like I told you two months ago, I have a modicum of Light talent." She frowned. "But the idiotic Temple rules in Issura wouldn't allow me to be placed there. None of the four clergy at Light are in any shape to assist you. Therefore, I volunteer."

I leaned back in my chair. "I appreciate your offer, but that's only putting a target on your own back."

She lifted her chin. "I'm willing to take that risk. Besides, who else could help you?"

I smiled. "You're not the only Issuran priestess with Light talent in the city. I was considering asking Sister Claudia of Love."

"Oh." My revelation seemed to take Leocadia back. "But isn't she still, um, recovering?"

"Yes, however—" I managed to resist laughing at her hopeful expression. "—I won't turn down an offer of additional assistance. I plan on consulting with High Brothers Jax and Talbert tomorrow after court about how to adjust the tracking spell to prevent another backlash. Would you like to join us?"

"Yes, I will be there." She stood, practically dancing in her enthusiasm. "Your investigations are so much more exciting than my regular duties."

"My investigations have a tendency to get people killed, High Mother," I said dryly.

"I promise to be careful and follow your lead, Chief Justice." She inclined her head while wearing a huge smile. "I'll see you at First Afternoon." Her step as she left my office was much lighter than when she entered.

Surprisingly, the voices didn't comment on Leocadia, and they remained silent for the rest of the night. However, I drank the soma tear in my milk as Master Bly suggested and warded my bedchambers when I retired. There was no sense in torturing poor Ming Wei with my nightmares.

⬥

Even more surprisingly, I managed to get a good night's rest for the first time since my mother returned to Orrin thanks to the soma tear. I presided over court the next morning, though Elizabeth attended as my truthspeller.

Chief Warden Nicholas had come to Balance a half-candle mark after First Morning, bearing High Brother Luc's apologies that none of the Light clergy could attend court. Nicholas didn't bother to dissemble when I bluntly asked him privately what was going on besides Shi Hua on bedrest and Garbhan not released from the Healers Guild yet.

In fact, Nicholas smirked beneath his facial hair. Apparently, Luc held a Temple meeting after he'd returned from Child and apologized to everyone for his behavior over the last two months. He gave Jeremy permission to sleep in this morning.

"Honestly, Lady Justice, the high brother had every intention of attending court himself today, but he got sick during the dawn services," Nicholas said.

I sighed. "Withdrawals?"

"Withdrawals," he affirmed. "The high brother refused to let Istaqa summon someone from the Healers Guild, but I spoke with High Brother Ben before I came here. He gave me an herb mixture to deal with the worst of the symptoms."

"Thank Vintner, Ben knows his business, but you know Luc will refuse to take the remedy," I said. "He seems intent on punishing himself for what happened to Claudia and the babe."

"Aye, that's why Istaqa is sneaking it into his food and drink." Nicholas sobered and shook his head. "Hopefully, High Sister Mya will make some headway with him as well. Thank you for your help, Chief Justice."

I made a self-deprecating sound. "I didn't help. I shouted at him for being rude."

"And that's what he needed, m'lady. A peer to speak the truth."

Nicholas stroked his beard. "Anyone of lower rank would have been lashed for saying what needed to be said."

"Chief Warden, if anything like this happens again, please tell me. None of you should suffer his cruelty, even if he was striking out in his own pain."

And I was the reason he was taking his grief and anger out on everyone else. I should have insisted Gerd be tried in Orrin for her crimes last winter. I could have recused myself and had the remaining ten Temple seats try her in banc. By her own admission, she had the damn grimoire in her possession with the intent to sell it. That was an automatic death sentence. It would have saved all of us the terrible events of this year.

We can show you how to manipulate time, the voices whispered. *Not just see it, but physically go back and change events. You could even go back and stop her from trying to abort you. Then, you could be the one to give Luc the child he so badly wants—*

"Chief Justice?" Donella, my senior clerk, said loudly.

I blinked. I'd been so caught up in replaying this morning's conversation I didn't notice Donella or Elizabeth approach my podium, much less that the disputants, witnesses, and spectators had left.

"I'm sorry. What did you say?"

"High Brothers Talbert and Jax and High Mother Leocadia have arrived for your meeting," Donella said. "Sivan has already escorted them to the receiving room."

"Thank you." I smiled at the young woman. "Would you please escort Chief Justice Elizabeth to the receiving room while I retrieve the evidence?" I made a point of using Elizabeth's full title out of respect for her former and future positions, but part of me wondered if she hoped to keep my seat in Orrin while I was banished to Tuqan Island. Far away from the mainland, and well away from any trouble. I wouldn't put it past the Reverend Mother.

"Evidence at the dining table, Chief Justice?" Elizabeth clicked her tongue. "That is hardly fitting etiquette."

"Most of my meals are working meetings these days, Elizabeth," I snapped. "And that's even when I have a chance to eat. If you don't wish to attend—"

"It wasn't a complaint, Anthea," she answered coolly. "Donella, I am ready."

My clerk called out steps as she guided Tandor's former chief justice down from the dais and out of the courtroom.

"Was that really necessary?" Little Bear asked from behind me.

I slid off my stool and sheathed my sword before I turned and looked at him. "And what exactly is your grievance, Chief Warden?"

"That the head of our Temple is not taking proper care of herself." He clasped his hands behind his back.

"I got a decent night's sleep for once," I said. "You and Sivan can relax."

"Only because Master Healer Bly prescribed a drop of soma tears in milk." He eyed me. "Tears can be even more of a problem than drink if you become dependent on them in order to sleep."

"One night does not constitute a problem." I turned and strode toward my office. However I should have known Little Bear wasn't about to let the subject go. His bootsteps followed mine, and he closed the door to my office once we were inside.

"I'm not Nicholas," he said through clenched teeth.

"I never said you were." I crossed to the wall where the Temple's safe hole was. My palm rested on the cool marble, and I muttered the spell to open the safe.

"Nor will I ignore a Chief Justice who is treating people in her Temple as rudely as the High Brother of Light has been treating the people in his," Little Bear ground out.

"Really?" I retrieved the silk bag containing the claw. "I don't recall telling Elizabeth or Yanaba they weren't allowed to ward their own damn quarters."

"Now, you're being deliberately obtuse, Anthea."

I whirled to face him. "No, I'm tired of everyone complaining when I'm the one who all the renegades have been trying to kill for the last year, including my own mother!"

Little Bear lowered his voice. "Luc and Claudia weren't the only ones Gerd harmed. That's why I think you should visit Child as well."

All my irritation drained away, leaving exhaustion in its wake. So much for my one good night of sleep. No doubt Sivan had enlisted her lover's aid in nagging me.

I sealed the safe hole before I slumped against the wall. "Then I might as well move into one of the Child's cloisters for those they can't cure, Little Bear. It's never been just one trauma for me. Between Gerd and the Reverend Mother, it's a wonder I haven't taken my own life."

I straightened. "However, I have no intention of either biddy winning in that way. Especially not by overdosing on soma tears. Master Bly said one night, and one night it will be."

Little Bear cocked his head. "And then you will return to exercise yard during the night hours, working until both you and Ming Wei are so tired you can't help but sleep?"

"Did she have nightmares last night?"

"No," he admitted.

"And how do you know?"

He smiled. "Mylon keeps an eye on both of you."

Of course, he did. So did whoever had the night watch with him.

"I'll make sure to ward my room again tonight," I said sourly. "Just in case. But for now, we have guests."

Little Bear opened my office door and gestured for me to exit first.

Hopefully, my next discussion would be more fruitful than the constant harassing of my staff over my mental and physical fitness.

Chapter 10

When I entered the receiving room, the other four clergy were already seated. Whatever intense discussion that was going on before Little Bear and I arrived abruptly halted at our appearance.

I decided to ignore their own rudeness. Besides, it was probably just Elizabeth complaining about me. She could butter the other seats all she wanted. They had no say in who held the chief justice position in Orrin.

"Have you all seen the rendition made of the creature based on the witnesses' descriptions?" I asked.

"Yes." Jax held up a piece of papyrus. "Clerk Leilani was kind enough to provide a copy upon our arrival."

"This is the broken claw Master Healer Bly found embedded in one of the victim's femurs." I held up the bag. "Brother Garbhan took a few shavings from it for his tracking spell. You all know what happened next." I circled the table to my chair and handed the bag to Talbert on my left before I flopped ungraciously on the seat cushion. "Any suggestions on finding this blasted creature without killing ourselves would be appreciated." I said the last with a direct look at my chief warden who took the chair to my right.

Talbert peeled back the cloth so he could examine the talon without actually touching it. "That's odd."

69

"What is?" I reached for the water pitcher instead of the wine. After seeing Luc yesterday, I didn't have the desire for anything stronger.

"Even with my senses, it exudes nothing more than a hint of animal." Talbert frowned and passed the talon to Jax before he turned his gaze to me. "Did you or any of the others detect anything out of the ordinary before attempting the tracking spell?"

"Nothing." I sipped my water. "Until it blew up in our faces. Then it definitely felt like demon magic."

Jax sniffed the talon. "The scent is close to a skinwalker, but not quite. Forgive me, Anthea, but it smells more similar to Gerd just prior to her death."

"No apology necessary." I waved my hand. "From any of you. With my sight, I could see she was in the initial stages of becoming a skinwalker."

When a human used demon magic, it changed them on a fundamental level. Their skin no longer shone yellow or orange to my strange vision. Instead, their skin turned a sickly grayish-green. The only reason the queen's cousin Samael DiRoy still looked human was because he hadn't actually cast a demon spell. He used human magic to summon demons to our plane. However, he'd been about to order the demons to wipe Duke Marco's memory of Lady Katarina when I stumbled onto them . . .

"I recognize that look on your face," Little Bear murmured. "What puzzle pieces fit together in your brain?"

I turned to him. "Who witnessed the destruction of Samael DiRoy's grimoire?"

The three men exchanged worried looks. Leocadia leaned closer to Elizabeth and whispered, "Who's Samael DiRoy?"

"One of the queen's cousins." Elizabeth chuckled. "I'll tell you that tale later."

I ignored the women and turned to my chief warden and demanded, "Tell me."

Finally, Little Bear said, "The Reverend Mother took it back to Standora for disposal. Surely, you don't think—"

"I'm not accusing her of anything." I made a sharp motion with my hand. "We know there's a spy at the home Temple. But if I could manage to create a volume and contaminate it with enough demon essence to fool a demon temporarily, why couldn't they and the renegades do the same to us?"

"It would explain why Yanaba was sure she had witnessed Gerd's grimoire being destroyed," Elizabeth said thoughtfully. "Did both grimoires look and feel the same to you?"

"I never saw or touched Samael's grimoire," I said. "His demons had already taken it to Lady Cora DiMara by the time they captured me. And I was technically under arrest after that."

"So Samael never looked like a skinwalker to you?" Talbert asked.

I shook my head. "For all his idiocy, he made sure to command the demons to cast the spells. He didn't have the talent to cast them himself. No use of demon magic, no contamination." I chuckled. "Considering how one of the damned things wanted to eat me, I don't think Samael touched them either."

"Maybe that's the key." Leocadia leaned her elbows on the table, and she seemed deep in thought.

"What key?" Jax asked.

"The demons' deepest desire is to consume everything on our world," she murmured. "What would happen if a human ate another human?"

A chill ran through me, and not just because of the taboo subject. The creature in the seamstress shop reminded Noko and Garbhan of a half-shifted Wildling. I turned to Jax, who looked as troubled as I felt.

"There are mentions in the Book of Wildling of diseases caused by eating your kin of the flesh." He ran his hands through his hair, making it stand even more on end. "There's a story of a man who's second form was a bear. He was tricked into eating bear by an enemy. The man became a twisted creature, and in turn, he ate his enemy. The Wildling God forgave him for being tricked, but there was nothing he could do to cure the creature. Nor could he allowed it to destroy the balance of the forest. He gave it to Death."

"So this could be demonic, or we could have something else entirely on our hands," Leocadia murmured.

"There has to be a reference to something like this somewhere more specific than scriptures," I said.

Talbert snorted. "Perhaps. Or perhaps it's like the prohibition on vegetation by the city walls. Our ancestors thought it was such common knowledge they didn't record why we needed to do it."

"All of this is an interesting history lesson, but it doesn't solve the problem of finding this thing," I said.

"We need to figure out how to destroy it before we find it," Elizabeth said. "Otherwise, we're borrowing more trouble, and we already have enough on our plate."

"May I?" Leocadia held out her hand to Jax. He gave her the silk-wrapped talon just as Sivan and one of the kitchen girls entered with trays of food. The way the high mother peered at the remnant made me nervous.

"What are you planning, Leocadia?" I demanded.

"Just a little experiment." She smiled. "Sivan, can I trouble you for a clean, empty plate?"

"Of course, High Mother." My head of household handed Leocadia a plate from the stack on the tray she carried before she and the serving girl set down bowls of cheese, bread, and fruit for our midday meal.

"Wait a moment here." I held up my hands. "What exactly are you going to do? Because just a few shards from that talon tossed me halfway across Light's sanctuary. I don't feel like repeating the experience twice in less than a day. Not to mention landing on my temple's marble is going to hurt a lot more than Light's wood."

"Which is why I'm going to have Talbert ward a section of the table." Leocadia looked up at Sivan. "May I have a second plate? I'll use it as the roof and goblets as the walls—"

"Wait just one moment, High Mother," Sivan blurted. "I can't have you destroying Balance furniture and dishes. I finally managed to replace the essentials after Justice Yanaba had to cast the Temple's last resort spells last spring."

"I have a better idea," Talbert said. "If we're going to experiment, I suggest we do this either outdoors or down in one of Balance's gaol cells."

"Perhaps it would be even better to perform this experiment in the Temple of Mother." Jax wore a wicked grin.

"Are you trying to provoke a fight?" I asked.

"At times, I enjoy poking a den to see what comes out." It didn't seem possible, but the Wildling's grin widened.

"I don't care where you do this experiment, but I'm not cleaning up the mess," Sivan snapped.

Our three guests stared at my head of household with various expressions of surprise and dismay that a staff member of a Temple would speak thusly to clergy. On the other hand, Elizabeth laughed loudly, and even Little Bear and I snickered.

"It would seem all of Balance has picked up Anthea's bad habits," Talbert said. "Very well, Mistress Sivan. We will endeavor not to destroy any of your furniture or dishes. We'll take our experiment down to the gaol."

"Triggering demon magic in an enclosed underground space in a Temple," Jax grumbled. "Nothing could possibly go wrong with that."

Chapter 11

We ate quickly, and I returned the rest of the talon to the Balance safe hole before we trooped down the winding staircase to Balance's gaol. I insisted Elizabeth remain behind. There was no sense in both of us getting killed when Leocadia's experiment blew up in our faces.

In the back of my mind, the dead demons chittered with excitement. They said they would protect me from the embedded demon magic in the creature's talon. They became quiet when I silently asked them why they didn't protect me yesterday afternoon.

Was that the secret to succumbing to the demons? One had to willingly submit to their requests? So why was it acceptable to eat a human without asking, but they needed our permission to work their seduction? I set aside my unanswered questions, not that I expected truthful answers from the voices, and focused on the tasks before us.

Despite their own wardens' protests, the other three seats commanded them to remain in the courtroom. When I pointed out there was no need for Jax to accompany us, he proclaimed there needed to be a witness to our idiocy.

When the other Temples' wardens questioned why Little Bear was allowed to go down to the gaol, I said, "My Temple. My rules."

"Besides, he's as stubborn as his chief justice," Jax commented.

"And High Brother Jax will need someone to confirm his story when those three get themselves killed," Little Bear added.

Prior to going downstairs, Leocadia shaved one tiny piece from the talon with her own dagger. She covered the plate and shaving with a clean napkin Sivan provided. It was cotton rather than silk so Leocadia handled the ceramic even more carefully than one would expect.

Once we were in the gaol proper, I wondered if it was such a smart idea to be experimenting with demon magic so close to the hidden grimoire. What if the talon and the book fed off each other somehow? I could be making a bad situation even worse. But if I protested now, it would arouse the others' suspicions.

Luckily, we hadn't had a major brawl in the city now that the weather was a little cooler. Therefore, our goal was empty of any prisoners.

"So how are you planning to manage this test of yours?" Talbert asked as he assisted Little Bear with removing the spell-threaded manacles from the one cell that wasn't equipped with a sleep slab or an oiled wooden bucket used as a chamber pot.

"Considering what happened to poor Brother Garbhan, I believe the demon spell targets our type of magic," Leocadia said. "More specifically, Light magic. It's why all the clergy were affected, Brother Garbhan worst of all, but none of the wardens."

"My wardens who were there aren't talented, not even passive talent," I said. "Neither is Warden Yar."

"Brother Sisquoc said the wardens from Father and Conflict present were also non-talented," Jax commented.

"Garbhan said one of the symbols the creature formed with the limbs was the ancient one for 'priest,'" I said. "He also suspected it may have been casting a spell using the limbs."

"So something specifically directed at us?" Leocadia fingered the hilt of her dagger. "Maybe it left that piece of talon intentionally. A way to take out you and any Light priest assisting you."

"It wouldn't be the first time," I growled.

"What exactly is your plan, Leocadia?" Talbert asked as he and Little

Bear set the chains in the adjoining cell. He strode out into the hallway. "My wards are going to prevent the tracking spell from completing."

"If I can get the demon spell to play out using a different Light spell without destroying the shard, we could then use it for a tracking spell." Once again, she seemed rather pleased with herself.

"But that means you being within the wards," Jax protested. "That's a good way to get yourself killed."

"Not if Anthea freezes time around my spell." Leocadia waved her hands dramatically. "The instant Talbert throws up his wards, my Light-related spell will be released from Anthea's time freeze and trigger the demon magic in the talon."

"With all due respect, High Mother, how did you come to that conclusion?" Little Bear stared at her.

"Actually, Anthea inspired it." Leocadia's face brightened to orangish-red. "I read your account of how you and one of the Diné Light priests manipulated time to get a Jing flashbang into the Tandoran tunnel system without opening the passage while demons were in it."

"That was sheer desperation in the middle of a siege!" I threw my arms into the air. "We were damn lucky!"

"The theory is still valid," she protested.

"We can stand down here all afternoon and argue, or we can try this insane plan," Talbert grumbled. "I don't know about the rest of you, but I have quite a bit of work to do if you all wish to continue debating the merits of this mad idea."

"All right, but how do we not set off the demon spell while preparing for Leocadia's crazy plan?" I asked.

"Ward the shaving before hand," Little Bear said.

We all stared at him.

He shrugged. "From everyone's reports, the demon magic wasn't triggered until direct human magic acted upon the talon. Otherwise, it would have been set off by the chief justice's rewind spell."

Jax laughed. "Be careful, Anthea. Little Bear might just replace you."

"He can have the seat of Balance," I said at the same time my chief warden shuddered and said, "You could not pay me enough to be chief justice."

"If you would, Leocadia?" Talbert gestured toward the cell.

She went inside, carefully set the plate on the stone floor, and removed the napkin that covered the shaving. Once she exited the cell, Talbert muttered under his breath. A sensation akin to kitten paws kneaded my skin.

"So far, so good," he said.

I looked at Leocadia. "What next?"

"I'll create an illumination ball that will extinguish itself in two heartbeats," she murmured. "Ready?"

I nodded. Leocadia held up her hands and whispered to herself. I couldn't see a light ball the way everyone else who was sighted could. The light it produced didn't give off enough heat to distinguish it from its surroundings. But I could feel the prickle of its magic along my skin, just like I could feel Talbert's warding.

With a sharp tug, I stopped time from moving forward around Leocadia's ball. "Drop the wards, then get back."

Little Bear ducked into the closest cell, but Jax had to drag Leocadia in with them.

I manipulated the frozen bit of time until it hovered over the shard without touching it. Sweat formed on my forehead and a drop trickled into my left eye. I blinked away the stinging sensation.

"I'm pushing the light ball down." I swallowed hard. "That will give us an instant between me releasing time and you getting your wards back up before the ball touches the shard."

"On your word," he murmured.

"Now!" I released time. The wards reformed in the cell. Talbert yanked me into the adjoining cell along with the others.

There was no sound of breath. The others must have been holding theirs as I was. Two heartbeats passed. Three. Four.

Carefully, we all peered around the edge of the cell's doorjamb. I looked at Talbert beside me. "Did anything happened?"

"No." he grimaced.

I straightened, strode over to the warded cell, and held out my hand. Time passed in its normal manner within Talbert's spell.

"Well, that was a spectacular failure," Jax remarked.

"I thought for sure it would react to Light magic." Leocadia folded her arms over her chest and frowned.

"That's because the light didn't act on the shard any differently than the lamps." Little Bear gestured at the sconces along the aisle. "I don't suggest another tracking spell, but what if you used magic to heat it without destroying it?"

"That's doable." Leocadia nodded.

I took a deep breath to calm myself, but the voices whispered dire imprecations in the back of my mind.

Which meant we were on the right track with Leocadia's experiments.

"Ready?" she asked.

"Do it."

"Same as before," she murmured. This time, I had to squint against the brightness of her spell. The energy she poured into the ball made it nearly as hot as our kitchen oven. It made the spell visible to me, but not the others. Though from the green sweat on Leocadia's face, she felt the effects.

Once again, I froze time around her spell. Talbert dropped his wards on the cell, and I nudged the frozen time into place.

"Now." I released the time. The wards snapped back into existence inside the cell. This time, I didn't need Talbert. I was already jumping for shelter.

He cried out, and the frigid wind I'd felt in Light's sanctuary yesterday swirled in our hiding place.

Little Bear caught Talbert as he started to go down. Then the rush of air blew out every single lamp in the gaol.

Chapter 12

"Is everyone all right?" I called out. There was no headache like I had yesterday, but there was definitely a metallic taste in my mouth. Talbert had taken the brunt of the demonic backlash. Little Bear cradled the unconscious priest on the floor. Above us, Balance's bells tolled the demon alarm.

Light magic tingled, and Leocadia said, "That's better. Oh, dear!"

Beside her, Jax had shifted into his wolf form. It must have been an unconscious reaction to the demon magic because he still wore his clothing.

Talbert groaned. "Did someone recognize the horse that ran me over?"

I stepped into the corridor. This time, the warmth of Mother magic brushed across my skin as Leocadia followed me and relit the gaol lamps.

Elizabeth, could you please silence the alarm and extend my apologies? Of course.

I could feel her laughing along with the other voices in the back of my mind. All of them irritated me. The whole point of Talbert's wards was to keep the demon magic contained. Maybe I put too much faith in his quicksilver nature to protect him.

Bootsteps thundered from the direction of the winding stairwell.

Gina and a handful of Balance wardens jogged around the corner into view. All of them were armed to the teeth.

Gina skidded to a halt in front of me and blinked at the sudden brightness. "What in Balance—"

Little Bear stepped out of the cell with Talbert, the priest's arm slung over my chief warden's shoulder. "Would a couple of you assist the High Brother to the couch in our receiving room? And please summon a healer."

"I'm fine," Talbert grumbled. "I don't need a healer. I just have a bit of a headache."

"Considering what the demon magic in that damn talon did to poor Brother Garbhan, you are going to let a healer check your heart," Leocadia scolded. The flapping of her robes was reminiscent of a mother hen's wings as Dezba and Tahoma sheathed their weapons and slung Talbert between them. Leocadia chased them up the steps.

When they disappeared around the bend in the stairwell, Gina turned back to me and sheathed her own sword. "Should I even ask?"

I shrugged. "We were looking for a way to do a tracking spell on the damn creature that left body parts in a perfectly good seamstress shop."

"Anthea?" I turned around.

A human-formed Jax stepped out of the cleared cell we'd used for our experiments. He held the plate with the talon shard. A wide grin split his face. "I think Leocadia's idea worked."

In the Balance reception room, Master Healer Bly fluttered around Talbert as much as High Mother Leocadia. The healer doubled-checked his internal organs, but since Little Bear caught the priest as he fell, there were no bruises or cuts for her to deal with.

Bly snorted. "You four were damn lucky your experiment only ended with one aching head, instead all of you dead."

"But it worked," I protested.

I was saved from Bly's tongue lashing by Sivan bustling in with a tray that contained a steaming pot of tea and cups for everyone.

"Sivan, could I add something to Talbert's cup before you pour tea into it?" Bly asked.

"Of course." My head of household handed an empty cup to the healer before she poured everyone else's drinks.

"I don't need anything," Talbert protested.

"The reason for your headache is the heightened pressure in your blood vessels," Bly said as she measured a powder into the cup she'd requested. "Increased vessel pressure is not uncommon in those with Old Continent ancestry, but I want to get yours down before it triggers a brain storm." Her analysis quieted the High Brother of Thief.

Bly handed the cup to Sivan. "Add a little honey to it if you please, Sivan. The medicine I'm using is quite bitter."

Talbert grimaced, but I had the impression his attitude concerned the added sweetener, not Bly's fussing. Like me, he preferred his Jing black tea plain.

"So do we try the tracking spell next?" Leocadia asked once Talbert sipped his doctored tea.

"No," Jax and I said at the same time.

"It's too close to First Evening," Jax added. "I'm not risking non-Wildlings on a night hunt, and we're definitely going to need as much help as we can manage." There was a burr of anger in his tone, and I could guess why.

"Talk to Han and Jerrod," I said. "They'll want to be in on the hunt as well."

Talbert waved his free hand. "Not just them."

A wicked smile crossed Leocadia's face. "My Temple will assist, too."

"High Mother—" I began.

"Anthea, I may be able to clean house in regards to my wardens, but these women need to learn that being Temple means protecting all humans." Leocadia picked up the parchment with Leilani's drawing of the creature still lying on the dining table. "And with something like this, it's going to take all the Temples working together."

With a plan to start the hunt for the creature tomorrow, I retired to my office to catch up on the dispatches from Standora. The bells had finished tolling First Evening when there was a knock on my door.

At Dezba's essence, I called out, "Enter!"

She opened the door and poked her head around the edge. "Magistrate DiCook and a farmer called Kele wish to speak with you."

"Let them in." If it had been DiCook by himself, I would have suspected an excuse to dine here, but he brought someone else, which meant this was important.

The two men entered, and despair from the farmer raked across my mental shields. DiCook didn't bother with any niceties, which killed any of my desire to tease him about waiting to be formally announced.

"Chief Justice, Farmer Kele from Eagle Reach identified one of the women as his daughter," DiCook said.

I turned to the farmer. "I grieve with you." For once, the words weren't social etiquette. This blasted creature had killed and eaten five people. "Please take a seat."

After DiCook and Kele sat, the farmer said, "I know you probably don't remember me, but you showed mercy to my brother."

I smiled. Sometimes, Balance's memory exercises came in handy. "Hania wasn't it? Nine years ago when I was still on circuit?"

Kele nodded.

"How is he these days? Hopefully, he learned his lesson about courting more than one woman at a time without sharing the knowledge with the women in question." The lighter subject eased the pressure of his despair against my mental shields.

Kele managed to chuckle. "I told him he was lucky you didn't order him unmanned for how he treated those girls."

"Did he finally pick one of them?"

"No, and none of the woman in Eagle Reach would have him after that stunt. Our parents arranged a marriage with a woman in Redwood Grove."

His grief came back in a rush. "In fact, my daughter Pavati was supposed to go his home to assist with the birth of his fourth child. She left my farm a fortnight ago."

Tears trickled down his face. "She never arrived. Search parties from both villages scoured the area between, but we found nothing."

"He recognized Pavati as the third girl brought into Barbora's home," DiCook added.

"What about the local clergy?" I asked. "Didn't they try a tracking spell on Pavati?"

"Yes, but it resulted in the death of Brother Caleb of Wildling." Kele swiped the backs of his hands across his cheeks. "Which is my other purpose in Orrin, to deliver the news to the Wilding high brother. When Father Blue Feather tried to find her, the spell didn't work. He said it meant she was—she was gone."

"What did each priest use for their tracking spells?" I asked.

"They both used hair from her comb." Kele frowned. "Why?"

I ignored his question, stood, and crossed to the textured map of the duchy on the western wall of my office. "When did they each perform their spell? The day and time?"

"Brother Caleb tried on Fifth Day last week after all the search parties returned on Fourth Day without finding a trace of her. It was shortly after dawn," Kele said. "Father Blue Feather tried the following afternoon."

I swallowed hard to clear the bile from the back of my mouth. Father Blue Feather's tracking spell failed because Pavati had been eaten shortly before First Night. But if she were still alive the day before, where had she been for over a week?

I ran my fingers over the contours of the map. Given the creature's observed height and strength, it could have easily carried its victims here. Where had it kept its victims? I crossed my arms as I teased out the clue I was missing.

"What are you thinking, Chief Justice?" DiCook said.

"Our creature collected its victims on its way to Orrin." I tapped my chin with my forefinger. "We humans would have to stick to the roads, but with its size and shape, the creature is not so impeded. It would make better time."

"If it were wearing a human skin—" DiCook started.

I shook my head vigorously. "That's a supposition on our part based on the reason folks living in the Craft District didn't notice the creature or report a sighting. It could have just as easily used a glamour."

"Creature?" Kele looked from me to the magistrate and back again. "What creature?"

My shoulders sagged. "I'm sorry, Farmer Kele. An unknown being that uses demon magic may be responsible for your daughter's death."

His expression steeled. "I wish to join the hunt for this creature of yours."

"No." I held up my hand when he opened his mouth to object. "I understand your feelings in the matter, but thing is probably responsible for killing your Wildling priest Brother Caleb, too. Our Brother Garbhan of Light also tried a tracking spell on the creature after we . . . discovered the partial remains of your daughter and four others. It very nearly killed him. I won't be responsible for your family losing you as well as Pavati."

Kele bowed his head. "In other words, I cannot take her home for a proper burning."

"I'm so sorry, but the answer must be no." I glanced at DiCook who nodded. "Why don't you join us for the evening meal? Afterward, the magistrate will escort you to Wildling to make your report concerning the loss of Brother Caleb, and then you can go to Death to possibly identify your daughter's remains. High Brother Xander will do everything in his power to give Pavati a proper send off."

"I need to find lodging first," Kele murmured. "I barely arrived before the city gates were closed for the night."

"Come back here." I crossed to him and laid a hand on his shoulder. "You are more than welcome to spend the night here while you deal with matters at the other two Temples."

"Your offer is too gracious, Chief Justice, but I couldn't impose—"

DiCook nudged the farmer with his elbow. "Take her up on her offer, Kele. You're not going to find a better cook in Orrin than Deborah here at Balance."

"You've helped me a great deal." I smiled. "More than you realize. Please allow me the honor to return the favor."

"You give me far too much credit, m'lady." His skin deepened to a golden orange in his embarrassment.

Yes, I probably was. The way everyone dumped their emotions on me, I should have been assigned to Child. Retreating to one of their cloisters for the mad was beginning to sound like a better and better option.

After feeding DiCook and Kele and sending them on their own errands, I retreated to my office once again. The voices mocked me for showing generosity to the farmer when they weren't clamoring how tomorrow's tracking spell would fail. It made it harder and harder to focus on the case documents I tried to read. I finally gave up a candle-mark after Second Evening and retired to my bedchambers.

I wanted to slap Sivan and Little Bear's smirks off their faces as I passed them in the hallway. However, I simply didn't have the energy. Last night's sleep hadn't recharged my resources as much as I thought.

I stripped and climbed under the single sheet, but my feet were chilled. I got up and grabbed a blanket from the storage chest. I lay down once again, but a divot in the ticking bent my leg at an uncomfortable angle. I got up and pounded the ticking with my fists until it evened out. I flopped onto my bedding, but I found I needed to repeat the pounding on my pillow to even out the down. Normally, Sivan took better care of my room. I needed to have words with her in the morning.

The Temple bells started tolling five heartbeats after I'd finally found a comfortable position, but it wasn't the time they called. I rolled off my bed, already donning my discarded clothing as I listened to the pattern.

A demon attack at the Temple of Death.

Chapter 13

Ignoring my robes, I grabbed my sword and dagger and raced for the main doors of Balance. Bootsteps pounded on the marble as my wardens followed me.

As my bare feet hit the cold cobblestones of the thoroughfare, a scream of pain echoed down the street. The odd thing was the absence of any sounds of battle. Somehow, I slung on my harness while at a dead run.

I met Sister Nina of Vintner at the bottom of the steps to Death, and we both raced up them, two steps at a time. No warden stood on the portico, in itself a bad sign. I drew my sword as something burst through Death's lacquered double doors.

Frigid air swept past me, cold as a mountain blizzard. The creature itself was various shades of purple, gray, and black. Not the ultimate black of a demon, but close enough. It looked exactly as Noko and Garbhan described from the rewind yesterday morning. One of its giant hands held a bag slung over its shoulder. Entrails dripped from the talons of the other hand. Its stentorian bellow was somewhere between an angry bull and a mountain grizzly.

The creature started to swing the bag toward my head, but I was already diving. Air smelling of rotten flesh whistled past my ear, and I slid on the marble floor of the portico to get behind the creature. Nina wasn't as lucky. The bag struck her temple and slammed her head into the half wall that guarded the edges of the steps and the portico. She dropped like the proverbial sack of potatoes and tumbled down the marble stairs and into the Vintner wardens.

I rolled to one knee, and with a two-handed grip, I swung with all my strength, aiming for what should have been the tendon that connected the calf muscle to the heel of its right leg. The crack when I struck didn't sound like bone. No, it sounded more like when the winter ice breaks on Lake Tulamniu. The creature bellowed again, but this one was obviously rage.

Worse, I couldn't pry my sword from its leg.

I half-rolled, half-somersaulted to gain some room and my feet. The wardens converged and distracted the creature from me, but it used the sack as a mace. With the creature's longer reach and height advantage, the wardens couldn't get close enough to strike.

Help wasn't coming from inside Death. I could see three bodies on the floor. Two of them were still alive, but they wouldn't be for longer if the healers couldn't get to them. I stepped closer and launched one of the kicks Shi Hua had taught me. My bare heel meet the creature's right knee.

Crack!

Cold so bitter it burned blazed through my foot. It felt as if every one of my bones had broken. No, not broken. Pounded into meal. I screamed and collapsed to the portico floor.

Through my tears of pain, I watched the lower right leg of the creature break off. It tumbled down the steps of Death, taking Ahiga and two Vintner wardens with it. The lower leg simply melted and ran down the steps. Released, my sword clattered against the stone floor of the portico.

"Clear!" High Mother Leocadia's voice rang out. "Fire!" The sharp twang of bow strings followed.

Magic tickled and pricked my skin. I crawled over to a bench by the half wall and pulled myself up. My right foot had gone numb, but I feared putting any weight on it. Instead, I propped my knees on the bench and my elbows on the half wall.

Below me on the street, priestesses from Mother and Love lined the street in two rows. Except for High Sister Dragonfly, the sisters of Love dressed in full armor and knelt in front of those of Mother. The *berda*'s height would have made her stand out without the symbol of Love on her chest. She was positioned at the opposite end of Leocadia's line. All the women were armed with bows and full quivers. Leocadia kept her promise of kicking the members of her order into action.

Ahiga and one of the Vintner wardens used the half wall as cover. The other warden lay at the foot of the stairs, his neck at an unnatural angle.

The creature stood in the middle of the thoroughfare with burning arrows lying on the cobblestones around it. I blinked as my mind tried to process my sight. No, the creature definitely stood on two legs again. But how?

Clergy and wardens lined the side streets in case the creature bolted away from the archers. A block behind the priestesses, the priests of Father along with their wardens and Light's formed a secondary line of defense. Something was wrong, and I couldn't quite place it through my pain.

"Arm!" Leocadia shouted. The priestesses nocked their arrows. Magic burned along my skin as the women charged their weapons. The heat of uncontrolled passion. The blaze that transformed raw ingredients into hearty meals. "Fire!"

The second flight of arrows struck the creature with sounds of ice cracking. Bits of flesh dripped from its body and splashed onto the cobblestones. It bellowed, and shook like a horse avoiding biting flies. The arrows dropped and clattered on the roadway.

Two rounds of magic-infused steel was enough for the creature. It whirled and raced down the thoroughfare faster than horses toward the Death Gate.

Little Bear knelt next to me as Master Bly examined my foot. High Brother Xander sat beside me on the pew in Death's sanctuary as her apprentice Simi stitched up the long gash on his upper right arm.

"Only minor injuries at Death's Gate," Little Bear reported. "The Smiths Guild and the Carpenters Guild will have their hands full with the repairs to the gate itself. The creature was strong." He shook his head. "It bent steel as if it were clay."

Bly poked a spot on my ankle that sent fire up my leg. I gritted my teeth for a moment before I could say anything.

"Please tell me the Wildlings aren't tracking the creature in the dark."

"All right. I won't."

"But?"

"High Brother Jax says they lost the creature's scent at Ripple Stream," Little Bear said. "The Wildlings are fanning out on the banks in an attempt to find it."

"Ripple Stream?" Xander exclaimed. "It was headed south. Why turn north?"

"Traveling through the woods and fields is much easier than fighting its way through the city to one of the other gates," Little Bear retorted. My sarcasm was wearing off on my staff.

Balance, help me. I knew how he received his information. I pursed my lips and glanced at Bly before I faced my chief warden again. "Why is Sister Shi Hua involved? I've already had my posterior chewed for enlisting Justice Yanaba on this investigation."

Bly smirked but said nothing. Instead, she closed her eyes. Warmth emanated from her hands, driving away the numbness in my foot.

Little Bear fidgeted, which wasn't like him. "The high brother of Light is assisting her."

I concentrated and reached out to the priestess. *Shi Hua, tell Jax to retreat. Neither of us wanted to hunt this thing in the dark to begin with.*

There was a pause before she relayed, *He agrees with you. The Wildlings and their wardens are on their way back.*

The warmth in my left foot turned to tingling and burning as Bly continued her ministrations.

Anthea, what's wrong? It was the first time I'd heard Luc's voice in my mind for over two months. His mental touch brought tears to my eyes. Or maybe in was the scorched sensation in my toes.

I forgot to put on my boots when responding to the alarm. The creature is cold. Damn cold. Colder than an actual demon. When I tried to break its knee with a heel kick, it was like licking metal in the dead of a mountain winter.

Bly intruded into our link. *I can verify the creature's effect. The Chief Justice had a severe case of frostbite in her left foot, but she'll be fine.*

Chief Warden Axton of Death exited the stairwell that led down to their morgue. He crossed the sanctuary and stopped before Xander. "You were right, High Brother. The only things missing from the morgue were the twenty limbs from the seamstress shop."

Bly grimaced. "And after all our work with Sister Raven Claw to match each limb to the five victims, too."

"But why in Death does the creature want them?" Xander mused.

"Maybe it was saving the tastiest parts of its meal for last," I said.

The four of them looked at me as if I'd lost my own brain. Maybe I had. I'd never been good at the social graces, and I would be the first to admit that my sense of humor was rather dark. The voices snickering in the back of my mind didn't help.

I shrugged. "Sometimes, the simplest explanations are the best. Like any other predator, it thought it had left its meal in an undisturbed place. We moved the limbs. It became angry and took its meal back."

"That actually make sense," Axton murmured.

"It's disturbing," Bly protested.

"Why?" Xander asked. "Because they were human?"

"Yes!" Bly glanced at the hooded statue of Death. "We're nothing but fodder to the demons. This thing views us the same way."

Sister Raven Claw approached us. "Or maybe it simply wants to finish the spell Brother Garbhan suspected the creature was trying to cast in the seamstress shop." She reached into the pocket of her robes and pulled out a vial. "High Mother Leocadia and High Brother Han want your opinion, Chief Justice."

I accepted the small glass container. It felt terribly cold. I lifted the cork stopper from the vial and sniffed the contents. "It smells like water." I handed the vial to Xander.

He sniffed and nodded before handing the vial back to me. "Please tell me no one's tasted it, Sister."

Raven Claw chuckled. "No, we haven't. It's a few drops of the creature's leg left in an indentation on the street."

"So, I didn't imagine the damned thing's leg melting." I replaced the stopper and stared at its contents. "So why did the creature's talon remain solid in one of the victim's femurs, but the leg I broke melted when I kicked it and the limb broke off its body?"

"The water ran down the steps and then reformed into its leg," Little Bear commented. "It also lost quite a bit of its fur during the tumble down the Temple steps. The broken hairs also melted and reattached to the creature. What if it can change its state the way a demon can change its shape or density?"

I frowned as I stared at the water in the vial. There's was something I was missing here. The creature wasn't a demon. Neither its talon, its body, nor the vial of its melted form had the ugly gray-green of a skin-walker. Jax said it merely smelled similar to a skinwalker.

Anthea, can we talk when you're finished at Death? Luc asked, breaking my train of thought.

Luckily, my surprise was closest to the surface of my mind when Luc asked his silent question. But irritation was a close second, and I deliberately let the emotion seep into our link as I slipped the vial into the pocket of my robes.

About?

I don't think Chief Warden Nicholas is being entirely truthful in his reports to me of the events over the last couple of days.

I didn't have the energy to deal with Luc's pathetic moping, but for once, he wasn't drunk. And we both had our duties. He couldn't do his if Nicholas was selective in what information he fed Luc. On the other hand, Luc could simply be using Nicholas as an excuse to talk to me.

Well, if the High Brother of Light thought I would simply warm his bed again after the way he'd treated me for the last two months, he'd quickly learn how sadly mistaken he was.

Chapter 14

"Is Ahiga all right?" I asked Little Bear softly as we passed through the main doors of Death. The cold stone under my soles made me realize what a fool I'd been by forgetting my boots.

The warden in question rose from the same bench I'd used as an observation post. "I'm fine, Lady Justice." He shrugged. "Just some bumps and bruises. The healers have already taken care of me."

"Mmm-hmm." Little Bear glared at his junior warden.

Despite Ahiga's calm demeanor, his skin tone flared from golden to an orangish cast.

I shook my head. "As long as I don't get any complaints from the head of the guild, let it go, Chief Warden."

"I'm more worried about accusations of preferential treatment," he muttered.

"If that were the case, the entire city would be up in arms about the time and energy the Healers Guild spends on me," I retorted.

On the street, one of the Death priests stood with High Brother Ben as two other members of Death bound the body of the warden who'd died from a broken neck in the tumble down the Temple stairs.

I approached Ben. "I grieve with you."

"That thing wasn't a demon, was it?" Ben said.

"No," I admitted.

Ben frowned. "Then why was the demon alarm spell triggered?"

"That's an excellent question, High Brother." It was one I couldn't answer. At least, not yet, so I changed the subject. "How is Sister Nina?"

The high brother's muscles relaxed. "Chief Healer Aaron stabilized her before taking her to the guild estate, but she should make a full recovery."

I didn't know what else to say, and my headache from trying to ignore the demons jeering at me grew. It didn't help that Han and Leocadia approached us.

"If you'll excuse us, High Brother, we need to consult with the chief justice." Han's words may have been polite, but his tone brooked no argument.

Ben merely nodded before he clasped my right arm. "Thank you, Anthea."

I nodded and stepped aside so Han and Leocadia could spew about whatever crawled up their asses.

"I haven't conjured any answers," I snapped.

The two seats blinked, looked at each other, and faced me again. Even my wardens watched me with peculiar expressions.

"We weren't about to criticize the performance of your duties, Chief Justice," Leocadia murmured. "The high brother and I wanted to offer whatever assistance you needed in this matter."

Movement flashed in the corner of my eye. Talbert sauntered over to join us.

I groaned. "What do you want?"

"I was merely going to extend the same offer on behalf of my Temple and High Father Jerrod," Talbert said mildly.

"Jerrod still can't find his balls?" I sneered. The man infuriated me. All I did was try to save his reputation when I skated the edge of the law, and he'd resented me ever since.

"That wasn't called for, Anthea." Talbert didn't raise his voice, but there was an edge of sharpened steel in his tone.

I sucked in a deep breath while attempting to rein in my temper. "I apologize, High Brother. Despite Master Bly's best efforts, the last two days have taken their toll on me, and I have no right to take my issues out on the rest of you."

"Accepted." Talbert nodded. "I didn't see High Sister Mariana during the alarm. I was wondering if she'd found anything regarding the creature. I assumed she'd relay it to you with Brother Garbhan still in the care of the Healers Guild."

I pursed my mouth, trying to think past the noise in my mind. "Perhaps she relayed the information to High Brother Luc as Brother Garbhan's superior. It could be why he asked me to stop at Light before I retire to Balance."

That was what my instincts were trying to point out to me during the battle. I hadn't seen anyone with the badge of Knowledge on their shoulders while Leocadia, Dragonfly, and their priestesses attacked the creature or during the aftermath. The anger I'd tried to calm came roaring back to life.

"Let me confer with the seats of Light and Knowledge," I said as politely as I could manage. "We're already assisting the peacekeepers with extra city patrols at night, and the creature has retrieved what it wanted from Death. I don't think we will have anymore upsets before dawn."

Talbert wore his analytical expression, and I half-expected him to contradict me. However, he nodded and said, "I agree, Chief Justice. Good eventide."

"Good eventide." I inclined my head to the group before I pivoted and marched up the boulevard, the chill cobblestones reminding me I was still in my bare feet. Ahead of us, Dragonfly herded her priestesses and wardens back into their Temple. No doubt Love's staff kept any worshippers occupied and out of danger while the priestesses and wardens responded to the alarm.

They responded and Knowledge didn't. That thought stuck in my craw, especially after seeing at least two dead people.

"Did we lose any one else besides the Death warden and the Vintner warden I saw?" I murmured.

"No, m'lady," Little Bear replied. "We were extremely lucky."

I snorted. "You mean enough of Death was asleep so the creature didn't have a chance to slaughter them."

"If the creature could have gotten into the morgue without breaking the seal, it may not have killed anyone," Ahiga said.

"Seal?" I stopped in front of the Wildling Temple. "What seal?"

"High Sister Bertrice had a seal placed on the morgue door after the incident with Peacekeeper Dante and the demon eggs placed inside his family's bodies." Little Bear shrugged. "High Brother Xander has continued the practice and recommended it to all other of his order's Temples."

"Why didn't I know about this seal?" I protested.

"It was properly recorded by Justice Yanaba," Little Bear responded. "You happened to be in Tandor at the time, and from the pile of paperwork on your desk, you haven't gotten to it yet."

I started walking again, and my wardens quickly followed. "So the creature used a demon spell to break the seal, which in turn, set off the alarm spell." We'd reached Thief before I added, "Then why not break the alarm spell first?"

"Maybe it didn't know how," Little Bear ventured.

"Or maybe it isn't a sorcerer on its own," Ahiga said. "The demon spell could have been embedded in an object for one use. Either to disrupt the seal specifically, or disrupt any one Temple spell."

"That actually makes more sense." The post healing drowsiness was making it hard to think. The buzz of voices in the back of my mind sounded as if they were debating among themselves the merits of our theories of what happened tonight.

The Temple bells rang First Night as I and my escort mounted the stairs of the Temple of Light. One of the wardens whose name I couldn't remember past the weariness stood guard at the main doors. He frowned at my lack of robes and footwear, but he was smart enough not to comment on it.

"The high brother is awaiting you in his dining room, m'lady," the Light warden said as he opened the door for me.

"Thank you," I nodded as I entered the sanctuary and glanced around the huge vaulted room. The eternal flame still burned, and everything was back in its proper place. Unless one had been here yesterday afternoon, no one would know of the disaster of the tracking spell.

Old Edberth strode into the sanctuary from the hallway leading to the brothers' private quarters. He had been my grandfather's head of household when Kam was the Orrin high brother of Light. Rather than retiring to Standora, Edberth remained here to assist Luc in an unofficial capacity.

He bowed to me. "This way, Lady Justice." Unlike Istaqa, Edberth didn't object to my wardens escorting me. He merely beckoned us to follow him.

It wasn't like we didn't know the way, but any pleasurable informality was tossed out with the bathwater between the Assassins Guild's price on my head and demons on the loose again.

Well, and the fact today had been the first day Luc and I spoke with any civility in the last two months.

When we entered the dining room, a lavish spread lay on the table. Or lavish according to the time of day. Luc and Jeremy rose and bowed, a total reversal of both their attitudes after yesterday.

"Thank you for coming," Luc murmured.

"You had some questions?" I prompted as I sat. I didn't touch any of the foods though many were my favorites. I also made a point of taking a chair close to the door.

Luc schooled his face to a neutral expression, but his arms shook as he lowered himself back to his own chair. It was the only indication that his body was still trying to clear the alcohol from his system after he tried to pickle himself for the last two months.

"What is Brother Garbhan's real condition?" he asked.

Now, why was Jeremy here if Luc was accusing his chief warden of lying? Unless Nicholas wasn't telling any of the Light clergy the full story in an effort to protect them.

"According to the Healers Guild, the demon spell damaged his heart." I glanced at Jeremy. "But he also had a couple of broken ribs from the chest compressions. Master Devin said they would keep an eye on him for a day or two."

Jeremy made an "I told you so" grunt, but Luc ignored him.

"What happened at Death tonight?"

"The creature that killed five people and left their limbs in Dante and Barbora's shop went to Death to retrieve the limbs." I shrugged. "As for why it wants the limbs, we are still investigating."

"Creature?" Luc prompted.

I laid out the description my witnesses gave. "To me, it wasn't like anything I've seen before. Mainly purple, dark blue, and black with a smattering of green. It's cold. Colder than a demon's touch even. When I kicked it, I ended up with severe frostbite in my entire foot. It killed two wardens during its escape."

"Nicholas threatened to put us in chains if we left the Temple," Luc said.

The abrupt change in topic threw me off balance. "He what?"

"It was for your own safety, High Brother," Little Bear stated.

"You are not a Light warden," Jeremy spat.

"You're damn lucky I'm not," Little Bear bit out. "I wouldn't have put up with your load of horse dung for the last two months."

"How dare you—" Jeremy started to rise, but Luc grabbed his arm.

Jeremy sat, but from the look on his face, he wasn't happy about whatever Luc said silently to him. Instead, the younger priest cleared his throat. "Your point is taken, Chief Warden."

Little Bear didn't relax, but he nodded curtly at Jeremy's quasi-apology.

"You should know the wardens have already put together a plan to take Shi Hua, Yanaba, and Cedar Grove to safety should the need arise." I glanced at Little Bear and made every effort not to smirk. "My guess is they also have a contingency plan for you two and Garbhan beyond keeping you out of harm's way tonight."

"Is this your way of pleading leniency for Nicholas?" A small hint of Luc's old humor flashed in his eyes.

To my surprise, it burned my spirit far worse than the frostbite from the creature. I lifted my chin. "You have every right to have your chief warden lashed for threatening you, High Brother, but your entire staff, including your wardens and two of your clergy, are on the verge of mutiny. I wouldn't suggest you push them over the brink by punishing Nicholas for trying to hold this Temple together."

"You are taking his side?" Luc gaped at me.

I pushed to my feet. "My own staff and wardens managed to keep Balance running with a senile justice on the bench. Your staff and wardens have had to do the same thing with not one, but two drunken high brothers. They don't need us. We need them. Maybe it's time you got that through your thick skull."

I yanked the door open and left because I couldn't handle Luc seeing me cry over the fact I'd lost him. And he was simply the latest thing my mother had taken from me.

Chapter 15

I should have gone to bed and cried myself to sleep. Instead, I decided to save my bad mood for someone who deserved it. I strode back to my bedchambers and pulled on my boots and my robes. When I stalked back into the courtroom, Little Bear was relating the events at Death to Mylon and Jonata. Having to stay behind to guard Yanaba and Elizabeth, they'd missed all the fun.

"Where are you going?" Little Bear demanded.

"I beg your pardon?" I scowled at him. He could berate Luc all he wanted, but he'd better think twice if he was going to lecture me.

Little Bear scowled right back, but he did amend his tone. "Where are you going at this hour, m'lady?"

"To have a word with a neighboring seat."

"I do not envy you." He sighed. Maybe he was picking up my bad habits. "However, it needs to be done. Jonata, would you please accompany the chief justice? All I ask is that you keep her from killing High Sister Mariana without a proper trial first. I'll cover your watch until you return."

Little Bear's decision not to accompany me to Knowledge was surprising. He usually wanted to be at my side. Or maybe he was as tired of dealing with clergy who refused to perform their duties as I was.

"Yes, sir." Jonata nodded curtly.

I pivoted and marched next door to the Temple of Knowledge.

Being a handspan shorter than me, Jonata jogged to keep up. However, I knew she could keep her counsel in regards to whatever passed between me and another seat.

A pang of grief ran through me. These were the times I sorely missed Warden Tyra. She had the makings of a chief warden. Instead, she became another sacrifice on the altar of my life.

Again, the voices whispered they could bring her back. They could bring back all my loved ones. They could give me everything.

If only I'd listen to them.

I clenched my hands. Fingernails bit into my palms, sharp little bits of anguish. My entire life had been pain. Why should it stop now?

I stomped up the steps to the Temple entrance. The Knowledge warden standing guard at the main doors stared at me like I was mad. Maybe I was.

"I'm sorry, Chief Justice," he said apologetically. "The high sister has retired for the night. I'll make sure she knows—"

"I don't need Mariana," I snarled. "I need her damn library since my junior justice destroyed mine six months ago."

"B-b-but—" he stammered.

"And don't think I didn't notice none of you came to the Temple of Death," I added. "You do not ignore the bells tolling a demon attack."

His skin turned crimson. "The high sister said we should dismiss it. That it was another false alarm."

"She ordered you not to go?" Of all the stupid decisions Mariana could have made, this took the cake.

He stammered, realizing exactly how much trouble his entire Temple was in. If I called a convocation, all of the clergy and wardens would lose their heads. A demon attack was the worst possible circumstance. There was no excuse, no defense, and no exception for failing to respond.

"I changed my mind," I growled. "Wake your high sister. I'll be in the library."

The Knowledge warden turned a sickly yellow color. With an audible gulp, he opened one of the massive doors and gestured for me to enter. He called softly for an attendant. A young woman ran to him from the right side hallway. He whispered to her, and her color faded to the same sickly yellow as his skin before she scurried back the way she'd come.

Orrin's Temple of Knowledge had the same central rotunda design with corridors and rooms framing it on three sides. An ivory and gold statue of the goddess stood on a dais in the same position as the basalt statue of Balance in my own Temple. However, an open book rested on Knowledge's left palm while she held a lantern in her right.

Instead of bare walls, wooden shelves full of books and scrolls covered the marble slabs. The only bare spots were doors into other sections of the Temple. In the case of Knowledge, spiral staircases at the north and south walls led to the second-story balcony where even more records were stored. Wool carpeting covered the floor. Tilted tables and stools filled the area for those reading or copying works.

The Temple of Death had an Issuran university-accredited library thanks to High Sister Bertrice, the only place that came close to the breadth and depth of Knowledge. I always wondered if Bertrice had missed her calling or if she simply hated dealing with Mariana.

We can help you bring your friend Bertrice back, too, the voices whispered. *She sacrificed herself twice to save you—*

"Jonata, I need your help with the index," I said. If I let the voices continue, the tears that had been on the edge of falling all night would spill and possibly ruin the very tomes I needed. "It's not stamped in Balance code."

"Yes, m'lady." She grabbed a paper lantern from a stack near the entrance and activated the dormant light spell before she crossed to the massive book chained to the table directly in front of the statue of Knowledge. Unlike Light's magic, Knowledge light balls always needed something to contain them. At least, I wouldn't be squinting from a candle or oil lamp's heat.

Jonata hung the lamp on the metal hook attached the table and propped herself on the stool. "But you are going to have to tell me what exactly I am looking for here."

"Let's start with ice." I was thankful for the safety precaution of using light ball spells. This entire Temple would be nothing but kindling for a conventional flame. However, Knowledge light balls didn't have the same warm tingle as Light's did. It was more of an itch, and it made me feel like I was going to sneeze.

Jonata flipped pages to about a third of the way through the index. "Harvesting ice, removing ice, survival in an ice storm—"

I frowned. "Anything about a creature made of ice?"

She shook her head and looked up at me. "According to the chief warden, it used demon magic to break the seal on Death's morgue. Should I try the section of demons next?"

"Wait." I held up my right index finger. "Try the entries on skinwalkers first. High Brother Jax mentioned that's what the creature smelled like to him."

She turned the pages to the subject I suggested and made an odd sound in the back of her throat.

"What?"

"There are a couple of references back to demons, but nothing specific about skinwalkers." She shook her head. "It's almost like this was written by someone from Diné."

"I beg your pardon?" I gave her a stern look.

Instead of being embarrassed, Jonata chuckled. "You were born and raised in Issura, and you didn't have the benefit of stories from the homeland that Gina's grandmother told her."

My lips quirked at Jonata's analysis. "Unfortunately, you are correct in that matter." In fact, I had to rely on Warden Gina to teach me my birth father's language. Diné made learning the Jing language feel like a lazy walk to Bakers Street. And for all of the Diné language's elegance and multiple words for one simple thing, the Diné considered even broaching the subject of skinwalkers as a major infraction of etiquette.

I sucked in a deep breath, hoping the air would clear my mind. Or that's what I told myself anyway. "Are there any entries under cannibalism?"

A shudder ran through Jonata's slight frame. Cannibalism was one of the few taboos on which all peoples of our world agreed. She flipped some more pages.

"What in the Twelve do you think you are doing, Chief Justice?" an older female voice snapped. "And do you have any idea what hour it is?"

I looked up from the index book.

With a scowl, Mariana marched into the library escorted by her chief warden. Two other Knowledge wardens stood nearby, also frowning at me.

"I am well aware of the hour. But instead of sleeping, apparently, I must do your job as well as my own." I gestured at the index. "Brother Garbhan made a request for information from you—"

She waved her hands wildly. "It would be easier to do my job if you weren't dealing in demon magic and constantly raising false alarms."

I doubt she meant the insult, but my patience was officially gone. Mariana was of average height, which meant I towered over her. I used every bit of that height difference as I stepped forward. "Are you telling me that the murders of five civilians and two wardens isn't sufficient cause to find you derelict in your duties, High Sister? Or did Brother Garbhan insult you in such a way you decided to ignore those same duties?"

Her chief warden didn't make a move to intercede on behalf of his seat. Instead, he said, "Tonight's alarm wasn't false, was it, Chief Justice?"

"No," I ground out.

Mariana's skin turned a pale yellow, just like the warden at the main doors and the attendant.

"The creature Brother Garbhan inquired about broke into Death's morgue tonight," I continued. "It killed two wardens during its escape, and it nearly succeeded in taking out High Brother Xander and myself in the process. And given the number of attempts on my life this year, each one makes me exponentially more cantankerous as my wardens can attest."

An odd snort came from behind me, but I didn't take my eyes from Mariana.

She swallowed hard before she said, "We never had these types of problems in Orrin before you claimed the Balance seat."

"Is this how you really want to play the situation, Mariana?" I said. My rudeness would normally be inexcusable, but at this point, I didn't care. The wardens from Knowledge probably wouldn't have made a difference in the loss of two other wardens or the creature's escape tonight, but they still should have responded.

And from the testimony I'd heard so far, Mariana had deliberately refused to perform her own duties as a Temple seat.

She glanced nervously at her chief warden before she murmured, "What do you need?"

I gave her the same description of the creature I'd given Luc barely a half candlemark ago.

Jonata slid from the stool, and Mariana took the vacated seat.

"You mentioned cannibalism. If this creature who ate the civilian victims was human at one time, it was cursed by consuming its own kind," she said.

"By demons or the Twelve?" I asked.

Mariana frowned as she read something in the index. "According to the Books of Wildling, they are cursed by your own goddess to an insatiable hunger." She rose from the stool and marched over to a bookshelves on the eastern wall.

"According to Wildling lore, He puts the poor cursed creatures out of their misery," I retorted.

"Only if the consummation was unintentional." Mariana pulled a scroll from its slot. "Chief Warden, get me a lamp."

He didn't even give her a proper acknowledgment before he retrieved the lamp. I didn't need to truthspell him to know he resented his seat. But was it from forbidding him to go to our aid or treating him so poorly?

As Jonata and I followed the chief warden to the table closer to the shelf from which Mariana pulled her scroll, I noted he did not activate the dormant spell. His lack of action didn't seem to bother the high sister. Did that mean her chief warden wasn't a passive talent?

That in itself wasn't unusual. But the demon blowback from the tracking spell affected those with active talent. What would it have done to someone like Jonata? It was a purely intellectual question, but part of me wanted to put it to the test. Just not with my own wardens.

"This is a treatise by the Wildling Reverend Father Barak of the State of Athens of the Grecian League of States," Mariana recited. "'While there is no direct reference in the Books of Balance, taboos mentioned in other Books of the Twelve can be inferred as a sin against Balance Herself. These taboos violate the very order of the universe. Each taboo is mentioned in relation to the god who is governed with upholding the individual law. For example, the Books of Mother and Father both mention the taboo of incest, the Book of Wildling mentions the taboo of cannibalism, and the Book of Love mentions the taboo of relations between an adult and a child.'"

"What in Balance does this have to do with a horned creature made of ice that's running around murdering and eating people?" I snapped.

"Reverend Father Barak goes on to say that it is a justice's responsibility to bring those that sin to account before Balance." Mariana looked up at me. "He mentions the spark of Balance that created Light can be used to destroy those cursed by their sins."

I groaned and scrubbed my hands over my face before I met her gaze again. "High Sister, with all due respect, I am exhausted from battling a creature from my nightmares and having been healed twice in as many days. Could you please explain this to me as you would a child?"

"At this point, I would be guessing, Chief Justice." She grimaced and folded her arms over her chest. "The lightning you produced when you were lecturing the rioters on the South Side could possibly destroy the creature."

I shivered and rubbed my arms. "I haven't been able to replicate that event."

"Not to mention, we still don't know what this creature is," Jonata volunteered. "If it's using demon magic, the chief justice's lightning may not affect it anyway."

"I will do further research—" Mariana held up her hand when I opened my mouth. "In the morning," she added firmly. "You're not the only one that needs sleep."

"Is putting me off worth your head?" I snapped.

"And maybe these monsters are attracted to you because you're one of their kind," she spat back.

Jonata grabbed my wrist as I reached for my sword.

"You dare lay a hand—"

"Remember what Chief Warden Little Bear said before we left tonight," she said.

I took a deep, shuddering breath. While he'd been joking about me killing Mariana, I'd come close to doing something supremely idiotic.

My warden had saved me from myself, even if she had inadvertently saved the high sister's life.

When I relaxed, Jonata released me. Once again, none of the Knowledge wardens made a move to defend their seat. Over the last year, I hadn't counted Mariana as a potential threat. Maybe I had been so obsessed with my own birth mother, I didn't notice the danger next door.

"I expect a status report on your research by First Afternoon, High Sister," I said.

Mariana must have counted herself lucky I hadn't pressed the issue about her Temple's lack of response during the creature's break-in at Death. She inclined her head. "I will."

I whirled and headed for the doors. If I stayed, I don't think Jonata could have stopped me from taking Mariana's head.

Chapter 16

After thanking Jonata for her assistance, I contemplated my next actions as I wearily walked to my bedchambers. I should call a convocation on Mariana for failing her duties. If I did though, I would need to do the same for Luc's dereliction over the last two months. I couldn't play favorites.

My threat to him seemed to knock some sense back into Luc's head. Maybe my intimidation of Mariana tonight would have the same effect on her. We couldn't afford conflict between ourselves if we hoped to stop the ice creature, much less the demons.

I entered my bedchamber and locked the door. No soma drops for me tonight, but neither did I need to transmit my nightmares to Ming Wei. For surely after the events at Death tonight, I would have some once I fell asleep, and she didn't deserve to experience my own horrors. I concentrated and muttered the spell to ward my quarters.

A wave of dizziness swept through me. Between the healing magic hangover and running all around the Temple District tonight, maybe I'd be able to sleep soundly after all. It wasn't worth the risk of opening the safe hole. I fished the vial from my pocket and set it in a clean glass goblet on the large table I often used as a desk.

I flung my robes in the general direction of my wardrobe and flung myself onto my bed. While I was on circuit, I usually slept in my uniform at campsites, and I was too damn tired to undo the laces of my tunic and leggings. I did manage to kick off my boots before I pulled my sheet and blanket over me. However, as soon as my head hit my pillow, I was wide awake and staring at the blue and green patterns in the marble ceiling.

We know what the creature is and how to destroy it, the voices whispered.

"Of course, you do," I murmured aloud. "And what's the price for this knowledge?"

No price. It's as much a danger to us as it is to you. It must be destroyed.

"All I have to do is perform a demon spell to get rid of it, right?" I mocked.

Not ours. One of yours to find it. One of yours to destroy it.

"And I'm supposed to take your word for it?"

If you don't believe us, read the words on our backs.

A different kind of itch pricked my skin. The kind I had when I was about to spar with someone new. Someone far more experienced than me.

"No."

Then why do you keep us? Destroy us as we should have been when you seized us from the fools.

"Why didn't the Reverend Mother burn the grimoire you form when she returned to Standora?"

The odd chittering that was demon laughter rang through my mind. *You will only accuse us of lying no matter what story we tell you. Don't read us then. We'll relish your screams as the wechuge feasts on your organs, and eventually, a new master will find us.*

Finally. A name for the creature. However, I couldn't show my hand. "For all I know, 'wechuge' is a word you made up. It's nothing more than gibberish in any language I speak."

Read our backs, the voices repeated. *Discover the truth for yourself.*

Samael DiRoy hadn't been corrupted by his grimoire for simply reading it. After the initial summoning, he'd been smart enough to make the demons cast any other spells. Or dumb enough, which was why the demons had sought a deal with Lady Cora, the current duke's mother. She lost her head under the Reverend Mother's own blade for demon dealing and treason. However, the voices were so intent on getting me to read the grimoire they forgot one little thing.

"I can't read your backs. I'm partially blind."

You can see your own kind's dried blood, they taunted.

"And?"

What ink do you think was used on us?

A shudder ran through me and I curled into a fetal position under my covers. "There wasn't any human blood on the pages I saw." The ones I ripped out to create a fake grimoire. It felt like eons since that awful night.

We don't wish to be destroyed anymore than you do. The voices chittered again. *We are glamoured so only those we chose can read us.*

"No." My nails dug into the skin of my palms. "I don't believe you."

Your loss.

For the first time in the last two months, silence reigned in my mind. Quiet, blessed quiet, filled me. It gave me the chance to think logically.

Reading the grimoire probably wouldn't harm me. It hadn't harmed or corrupted Samael DiRoy. Temple laws didn't care about a human reading it when the penalty for simple possession was death. The contamination from touching the grimoire couldn't be seen by anyone but me. No one could access the new passage into the tunnels where I'd hidden the grimoire without entering my chambers. Therefore, no one could prove I possessed the grimoire.

While Mariana and her people would research the creature after our confrontation tonight, I couldn't be sure they would actually find anything worthwhile. I needed to know how to kill this wechuge. I had no control over the lightning I had produced before, nor could I replicate it. If the demon grimoire had a method to stop the wechuge that didn't result in my use of a demon spell, I needed to research it.

I glanced over at the goblet holding the vial of melted wechuge. Lightning would scorch a tree. How did we destroy something that would melt and reform?

Heat it until it turns to steam, the voices whispered.

Of course. How many clergy would it take to hold the wechuge long enough to boil it away?

The better question, why was I denying a source of information because of legal prohibitions. Orrin was my city. I no longer had the Reverend Mother dictating my every move. Twelve take her! My attempt to give myself sight allowed me to see the truth of demons, skinwalkers, and even this wechuge.

I pushed aside my covers, rolled out of my bed, and padded over to my new wardrobe. Warding the room meant Mylon and Jonata wouldn't hear me moving the piece. Thankfully, Sivan had replaced my old monstrosity with a smaller, lighter wardrobe after Yanaba destroyed everything in Balance along with the invading demons with the Temple's last resort spells. I'd never be able to move the old one in order to hide the new passage.

Once I shoved the wardrobe aside, I sat cross-legged on the floor and placed my palms on the marble block. Some concentration and a few muttered words. The block folded itself back, and I pulled out the grimoire.

The leather remained as black as the demons from which it was made. Now, I understood why I thought it cried out in distress when I ripped the pages out last winter.

"I'm sorry for hurting you," I whispered.

The voices crooned a wordless acceptance of my apology.

I opened the book. The first few pages were as blank to me as any other book. I turned the fifth piece of parchment and simply stared.

The pale symbols stood out on the black pages. Thanks to the sailing acumen of the Phoenicians, their alphabet became the basis of the trade tongue. It had been taught at the home Temple in Standora, even though Balance used its own system of raised dots and lines in order for the sisterhood to read through touch. The only way we could read the Phoenician symbols was if they were carved into something.

Even the odd sight I'd given myself couldn't discern ink from papyrus or parchment made from our own animals. But this? For the first time in my life I could read as my staff or wardens did.

That thought brought the tears I'd managed to quell all night to the forefront again. I quickly wiped them away with my sleeve. Balance only knew what kind of interaction my bodily fluids would have with the grimoire.

"All right. I'm looking at you. Can you at least tell me where the information regarding the wechuge is? Or do I have to shove you back into the hole?"

The voices whispered the number of pages to turn.

I swallowed hard as I turned to the appropriate section of the grimoire and I began to read. Mariana and Jax were right about how the wechuge came into existence.

Cannibalism.

The word for the wechuge came from Dane-zaa, an affiliation of tribes far north of Pagonia near the Inuit Nations. Love, compassion, loyalty, the very things that made us what we were, were obliterated by the wechuge's decision to eat another human's flesh. They became as evil and dispassionate on the outside as they were on the inside. They literally became ice.

Was that the reason the talon caught in the victim's bone hadn't melted? The wechuge needed the last five victims to complete the process?

I turned the page and continued reading. Extreme heat was necessary to destroy a wechuge, either by spell or conventional means. It had to be boiled away like a pot of water in order to fully destroy it. Otherwise, it would reform and continue to consume any humans around it. The entry went on to say the wechuge were as dangerous to the demons as they were to humans. The wechuge could and would kill demons because it viewed them as competition for their food source.

The voices hadn't lied. I set the grimoire back in the tunnel, used the reversal spell to close the block, and leaned my back against the wall as I considered my options. The first of which was I couldn't let the wechuge continue whatever it was doing.

But how did I present this knowledge to my peers? I didn't dare admit I read the grimoire, much less that I had it in my possession. Maybe I could question Gina about the similarities in the Diné and Dane-zaa languages. Then I could mention that one of the Cheyenne clergy mentioned a story he'd heard from Dane-zaa trader.

Yes, that would be a safe method to approach the subject with my wardens. And I could use that opening to prod Mariana and her clergy in the correct direction for their research.

I slowly got to my feet and stretched. Now, if only I could get some real sleep, I'd feel so much better.

Chapter 17

Despite the nightmares, I managed to get a little sleep. However, I was still awake before the Temple bells rang First Morning. I dressed in my loose practice clothing and padded through the quiet hallways to the back porch. Ming Wei waited for me in the practice yard.

"Did you have my nightmares again, young squire?" I asked. "I swear I warded my quarters."

She shook her head. "I had my own last night, Lady Justice. Shall we do our first forms for our warm up?"

Ming Wei and I started slowly and then picked up our speed with each form. She called out each one, repeating those I made mistakes on until I performed them perfectly. In a way, the girl reminded me of the weapons mistress at the home Temple when I was a novice. The voices in my head mocked and jeered at me for my sentimentality and for listening to a mere child.

We were half way through the first technique of the second forms when Ming Wei abruptly stopped.

I lowered my foot to the packed earth. "What's wrong?"

She looked around us, but other than the plants, the stable, and the fading stars, there was nothing else in the practice yard. "I thought I heard voices."

"Voices?" I cocked my head. The ones in my mind quieted.

She shook her head. "Never mind."

"Ming Wei." I knelt beside her. "I believe you heard voices. Can you describe them to me?"

A look of raw fear filled her features. "I don't want to leave Balance. I'll ignore them. I swear to the Goddess."

"You're not in trouble." I wanted to hold her, comfort her, but she could barely tolerate any woman touching her other than Yanaba. Men were definitely out of the question. If I tried, I could make things worse. "Nor are you leaving Balance. I need Justice Yanaba, and she needs you." I hesitated a moment, but it was best to be honest with her. "Did you know High Sister Mya asked that you be tested for talent?"

The girl shyly bobbed her head, but the grimace on her face said so much more.

"Why does that bother you?"

Hot yellow tears formed in her eyes and trickled down her cheeks. "I begged her not to."

"Why?"

She gulped air. "What if I don't have talent? What if I'm just crazy? I hear voices when no one's around."

I swallowed my own laughter. Letting it loose would only hurt the child further. "High Sister Mya would know the difference. That's why she asked me to make the formal request."

Ming Wei swiped at her tears with the backs of her hands. "If she's so sure, why couldn't she make the request?"

"Because you're a squire at the Temple of Balance," I said softly. "She followed protocol by asking me to make the request."

"But I don't want to get tested," she wailed. She flung her arms around my neck with such force I rocked back on my heels. But she was touching me, wanting comfort through physical contact, which meant Mya had made a great deal of progress in healing the girl's emotional state. I put my arms around her and hugged her tiny body.

From her surface thoughts, I knew what was really bothering Ming

Wei. And I hadn't touched her mind. She was projecting her fears to me. "I can insist Sister Shi Hua administer your test. Would that make you feel better?"

She loosened her hold on my neck. "But High Sister Mya said the high brother of Light would test me. I don't want to be alone with him. He-he—" From her ragged breathing, she was about to hyperventilate.

"Inhale with me," I ordered. She did so. "Now exhale." It took five repetitions of the breathing exercise before her little heart slowed its pounding against my chest.

"High Brother Luc would never hurt you."

"But he hurt you," Ming Wei protested.

This time, I did laugh. "Our . . . differences stem more from annoyances with each other. It's more like when Nathan ate the last almond pastry after Deborah promised it to you, and you didn't talk to him for a whole day."

"But the high brother smells like—" Sobs racked her little body, she tightened her hold around my neck once again. "—like the bad man who hurt me." Each word was a sharp knife thrust of accusation against the Jing noble who had bought her from her parents. It was a pity the man was already dead. He would have been the one instance where I enjoyed taking someone's head for their crimes.

"If it helps, I made the high brother take a bath."

Ming Wei sniffed and released me enough look me in the face. "You did?"

"Yes, and if he still stinks the next time you are around him, let me know."

"I will." She nodded solemnly.

"In the meantime, I'll see about the sister testing you instead of the high brother."

"Thank you, Lady Justice."

A cock from Mother crowed, and our own rooster echoed its welcome of the morning a heartbeat before the bells rang First Morning.

"Go get cleaned up before Deborah has the morning meal ready."

"Yes, m'lady." Ming Wei curtsied before she dashed up the back porch steps.

Part of me hoped she did complain about Luc's foul smell. I could call a convocation and execute the bastard.

If you really want to kill something, you could start with the wechuge, the voices whispered. *Besides, when he touches the child inappropriately, that is an even better excuse to kill him.*

Anger rushed through me. *Luc would never—*

Intoxicated humans often give in to impulses they would control when they were not intoxicated, the voices whispered. *You say we are the perversions, and yet we would never do to our young the things your species do to yours.*

The sad part was the dead demons were right.

A candlemark later, I had bathed and dressed. I forced myself to sit still while Sivan stood behind me and braided my hair.

"After we're done here, would you please have Deborah put together provisions for Kele's return trip to his farm?" I said.

Sivan paused in her efforts. "Kele?"

"The farmer who spent the night here," I prompted.

"Oh, yes, the one whose daughter was missing." Sivan resumed braiding my hair. "He didn't sleep here last night, m'lady."

"What?" I jerked around to look at her, making her lose her grip on my tresses. "Why didn't he stay here? He came to report a crime. There was no reason for him to spend any money to stay at an inn."

She palmed my cheeks and forced me to face forward again. "I don't know what to tell you, Chief Justice. He never returned. Didn't he leave with the magistrate last night? It's possible he stayed at the DiCooks' home or one of the other Temples instead. The other seats would have extended an invitation given the reason Kele was visiting Orrin."

My blood froze in my veins. I didn't bother to truthspell Kele because he was reporting his missing daughter, and I had met him years ago. Magistrate DiCook planned to take him to the Temple of Death after he reported Brother Caleb's demise to High Brother Jax. That meant Xander or one of the other Death clergy had shown Kele exactly where the leftover limbs from the victims were. In my pain from the frostbite, I hadn't thought to ask Xander about Kele's visit.

And according to the grimoire, the wechuge was originally human. It only turned to ice over the continued consumption of humans.

"Nathan!" I bellowed as I started to rise.

Sivan yanked my hair hard enough to slam me back onto my stool.

My squire shoved open my bedchamber door. "Yes, Lady Justice."

"Run to Government House. Tell the magistrate I must find Farmer Kele immediately. He never returned to Balance last night."

Nathan bobbed his head. "Yes, Lady Justice." Once again, he dashed off without closing my bedchamber door.

"Why do you need to speak to Kele again?" Sivan was unnecessarily rough as she braided. I'd obviously irritated her, but if I chided her, she'd refuse to help me with my hair. So, I let her have her little rebellion.

"I need to truthspell him about last night," I murmured.

Sivan paused in her task, for which my roots were grateful. "Truthspell him about what?"

"His whereabouts last night," I said grimly. "Because I think the creature may be mocking us."

From their laughter, the voices in the back of my head agreed with my assessment.

Chapter 18

Instead of simply giving my squire the answer I desired, DiCook accompanied Nathan on the walk back to the Temple. I'd barely taken my first sip of tea when they burst through my office door.

"What's this about Kele not returning to Balance?" DiCook demanded. Behind him, Noko mouthed, "I'm sorry."

Personally, I was glad she didn't have Mylon's temper. He scared the magistrate. Noko didn't. And I didn't need the headache of her punching DiCook in the nose.

Though I was sorely tempted to do so myself.

"You're lucky Warden Mylon isn't on duty, Malven," I said dryly.

"Don't change the subject," DiCook snapped.

"Thank you, Nathan." I smiled at my squire. "Why don't you go to the kitchen and get something to eat? And please close my office door this time."

His face turned bright orange, but he bobbed his head. "I'll try to do better, Lady Justice." He marched out of the room, quietly closing the door behind him.

"Kele didn't come back," I said softly. "I retired early last night, and none of the staff saw him after the two of you left. Given the chaos at Death caused by the creature's invasion, I didn't think to check on Kele until this morning."

DiCook stuck his thumbs in his belt and rocked on his heels, a sure sign of his own worry. "After he talked to High Brother Jax, I left him at Death. Brother Elu was consoling him over the death of his daughter. It didn't seem right that I be there. Grief is such a personal thing. Kele told me he was sure he could find his way back to Balance."

I swore under my breath. "In last night's madness, I didn't think to ask High Brother Xander either." I pushed to my feet. "How are your peacekeepers dealing with the situation?" I grabbed my harness from its peg and buckled it on.

DiCook grunted. "Compared to demons, they're dealing with the creature just fine. No serious injuries when it rushed the gate, thank the Twelve. You've got some volunteers from my peacekeepers and some of the duke's men when you and High Brother Jax go hunting for that thing." He cocked his head. "Are the rumors true? The thing melted and reformed after you broke off a leg?"

"Yes." I brushed past him and opened my office door.

DiCook scurried after Warden Noko and me down the corridor. "And you have no idea what it is?"

"I have a suspicion." I needed to be careful how I worded it, too. When we entered the courtroom, I turned to Noko. "Would you please get Warden Gina to accompany us?"

"Yes, m'lady." She strode across the floor and disappeared down the hallway to the staff and warden quarters.

"I'm assuming I'm on my own for court once again." Elizabeth entered the courtroom, her hand curled around Warden Tahoma's elbow. Part of me rejoiced she was actually comfortable with one of the men in our Temple. After the horrible things done to her in Tandor, I was beginning to question whether Mya's staff would ever make any headway in healing Elizabeth's emotional issues.

"I'm sorry," I said. "I should have spoke with you first—"

"Don't fret." Elizabeth grinned. "I already summoned Brother Jeremy."

"Has the Healers Guild released Brother Garbhan?" I asked.

"Yes, with the caveat that he remain on bed rest for another day," Elizabeth said before she and Tahoma both laughed.

"Are you going to share the joke?" I asked. My question only made Elizabeth double over with hysterics.

"Sister Shi Hua told Brother Garbhan he could stay in her bed so they could keep each other company," Tahoma said.

I covered my face with my palms. "Balance help me."

DiCook, however, roared with laughter along with Elizabeth.

I lowered my hands. "She shouldn't have done that."

Elizabeth swiped at her tears with her free hand. "Then Luc needs to start leading his Temple instead of drowning himself in wine."

Even a blind woman could see Luc's mistakes. And people wondered why I was so angry all the time, but it was better than wallowing in a vat of alcohol to numb the pain.

He hurts everyone around him, and you allow him to do so, the voices accused. *What will stop him from hurting the younglings when you allow them to go across the street for their learning?*

You're wrong, I shot back.

Thankfully, Noko returned with Gina at that moment.

Except Gina decided to provoke me by teasing, "Is something wrong, Chief Justice? You balk at even one warden as your escort."

"Actually, I have some questions for you, but I also need to consult with High Brother Xander." I beckoned her. "Walk with us while Chief Justice Elizabeth tries to regain control of herself before court."

"Yes, m'lady." Gina fell in step on my left side as we exited the courtroom.

"Something about the creature sounded vaguely familiar to me," I said while we descended the steps of the Temple to street level. "It took a couple days and a trip to Knowledge for me to realize it was a story one of the Cheyenne Light brothers told during the siege of Tandor."

"Why would you think I could help?" Gina frowned at me. "I don't speak Cheyenne."

"No, but you do speak Diné." I watched for wagons and horses as we set off down the thoroughfare. The city activity had increased with the break in the weather and the anticipation of the Vintner's festival in three weeks.

"Yes, and?" she prompted.

"He said the Dane-zaa of the far north and the Diné were distantly related. Have you ever heard the word 'wechuge'?"

"No, m'lady." She shook her head. "May I ask what prompted your question?"

"We were talking about skinwalkers, and he mentioned a similar story he'd heard from a Dane-Zaa trader," I said. "But this wechuge was originally human and allegedly corrupted, not from using demon magic, but from committing a sin of such magnitude that even the Twelve turned Their backs on him."

"Like cannibalism?" Gina said.

"He didn't specify, but it sounded like it could be any taboo," I answered. "If I had foresight, I would have asked for a more thorough description."

Gina pursed her lips before she said, "I could ask, but . . ." A wagon rumbled by us, but that wasn't the reason she let her sentence trail off.

I sighed. "I know, I know. If it is a forbidden subject, you won't get a straight answer."

"Not talking about the monsters in our world is a damn idiotic way for our citizens to die," DiCook blurted from behind me.

"No one's disagreeing, Magistrate." I looked over my left shoulder at him. "That's the reason I want to ask Kele a few more questions."

Gina shot me an odd look, but then her eyes widened slightly as she put the pieces together. She gestured at the Wildling Temple. "Should I ask—"

"Chief Justice!" Sisquoc jogged down the steps of his Temple. I paused and waited for him to reach us. "Our high brother and High Mother Leocadia are requesting your presence to begin the hunt."

"First, I have a question for you. Did Kele spend the night at your Temple?"

Sisquoc tilted his head. "The farmer who came to report Brother Caleb's death?" He shook his head. "The high brother extended the offer, but he said he'd already accepted your invitation."

"He didn't return to Balance." I turned to Gina. "Collect clergy and wardens from the other temples for the search. Inform High Brother Jax of my suspicions." I turned to DiCook. "Get as many peacekeepers as you can. I'll talk to High Brother Xander and Brother Elu." I set off down the thoroughfare.

"Wait!" DiCook rushed to catch up and grabbed the sleeves of my robe. "What about Kele?"

"He may be the creature we're looking for."

Chapter 19

Noko and I reached the Temple of Death. At the look on my face, Chief Warden Axton escorted me to High Brother Xander's office without any questions on his part. Sitting at his desk, the priest looked up from whatever he was reading. His pleasant expression faded at my scowl.

"Did the farmer Kele spend the night here?" I blurted without a preamble.

Xander's eyes narrowed. "No. What's going on?"

I laid out my suspicions. "The magistrate left him with Brother Elu last night."

All Xander had to do was look at Axton before the chief warden rushed from the office. Xander regarded me. "I hope you're wrong."

"So do I." I hugged myself.

Brother Elu raced through the open door of the office, Axton on his heels. "The chief warden said you needed to see me. That it was an emergency."

"The man you were ministering last night—" Xander started.

"Kele." Elu nodded. "His daughter was one of the creature's victims."

"When did he leave Death?" I demanded. "And where did he go?"

"I tried to encourage him to stay here because of the late hour," Elu said. "He refused. However, he seemed quite distraught, so I escorted him to Child shortly before Second Evening."

"Are you sure?"

Elu nodded. "The bells rang the time as I walked back here."

I turned for the door when Xander said, "Wait, I'm coming with you."

He reached for his own sword harness, but the movements of his right arm were still stiff.

"You should have let Master Bly heal you," I said.

Xander flashed a wry smile. "She was busy saving your foot, and her apprentice needed to practice her sutures. And if this Kele is the creature who ripped through my Temple last night, I will be involved."

"That kind of stubbornness will get you killed," I snapped. "Just like it did with Bertrice."

Except for the sudden inhalation from Elu, a deadly silence reigned in Xander's office.

A silence he broke with the words, "That was unnecessary, Chief Justice."

"I'm tired of being blamed every time a seat in this damn city does something idiotic and gets themselves killed," I bit back.

"I understand you are frustrated by the events of the past three days," Xander said in a low voice. "But I will not tolerate your tainting of my predecessor's memory when she saved your life more than once."

Maybe I was rude, but I couldn't handle my emotions if something happened to Xander. No, I couldn't handle Yanaba's emotions if something happened to Xander.

I sucked in a deep breath. "Please stay here, High Brother. If not for your own sake, but that of Justice Yanaba and your unborn child."

His face and hands flamed a brilliant crimson. "That is a low blow, Chief Justice."

"Then allow me to go in your stead, High Brother," Elu murmured. "Or Sister Raven Claw." He glanced at me. "While the Chief Justice's words were . . . indelicate—"

Behind me, Noko snorted, then coughed. I really needed to speak with my wardens about their attitudes.

"—you are still recovering from an injury. Please, we can't lose you, too, Xander," Elu finished.

The high brother's color faded to a dull orange. "All right, you may accompany the chief justice, but take a warden with you."

"I'll go with him," Axton murmured.

"Thank you." Elu inclined his head.

I turned to leave Xander's office.

"Chief Justice?"

I looked over my shoulder at Xander.

"This is my Temple." His simple statement said if I showed him disrespect again, he'd do more than file a complaint. Nor did I doubt he'd follow through. One did not become a Temple seat at such a young age without a spine of steel.

"Understood, High Brother."

I left Death with my escort stalking behind me. Traffic was picking up on the boulevard as the morning progressed. We walked at a fast clip to Child.

When we reached the portico, the warden on duty frowned. "Brother Turtle and a squad of our wardens went to meet you at Wildling, Chief Justice."

"I know what my orders were," I snapped. "I'm seeking a farmer named Kele from Eagle Reach. Brother Elu escorted him here last night when Kele was supposed to spend the night at Balance."

The left main door abruptly opened. Mya's head of household Makawee glared at us. "What the demon is going on out here? All the clergy can feel you through the Temple shielding."

"The farmer Kele. Where is he?" I ground out.

"Asleep," Makawee shot back. "He needed help and healing after learning his daughter wasn't just murdered, but eaten."

I pushed past her and the warden. Tapestries covered the wall of Child's sanctuary. Designs I couldn't see without looking through someone else's eyes. However, the details of the jade statue of Child Herself were clearly visible to me. Unlike the rest of Twelve, She was shown as a girl in the stage between childhood and womanhood with a dove in her right hand and a sheaf of corn in her left.

Makawee rushed in front of me. "You are out of line, Chief Justice! I will not allow you to disrupt—"

"I will deal with her, Makawee." Mya entered the sanctuary from the doorway leading to the second story stairwell. The head of household stepped back and bowed her head, but I didn't miss the ugly look she shot me from beneath her lowered lashes.

Mya stopped before me. "I understand you are in pain, Anthea, but I will not allow you to lash out at my staff or my wardens."

"A good lashing may be exactly what's in order." I pointedly looked at Makawee. Behind me, Noko audibly gasped at my words.

I whirled to face her. "Do you wish to join her, Warden?"

Noko stiffened. "No, m'lady."

I turned back to Mya once again. "I need to interrogate Kele. Now."

"On what basis?" Mya folded her arms over her chest.

"He's the creature that's been murdering people," I snapped.

Mya drew back. "Based on what evidence?"

"He didn't come back to Balance last night, and no one knows his whereabouts when the creature attacked Death last night," I snapped.

Mya cocked her head. "He was here all night. When I wasn't with him, one of my people was."

"This thing uses demon magic." I flung my arms in the air. Why in Balance was she arguing with me? "Gerd used the same demon magic to mess with High Brother Ben's mind."

"You may question him—" She held up her hand when I opened my mouth. "—but I want a third party casting the truthspell."

"What is that supposed to mean?" I ground out.

"You are the proverbial bear in a pottery shop when it comes to truthspells, Anthea." She lifted her chin. "I won't have you kill an innocent man based on some subjective whim."

I gaped at her insult. "I'm trying to stop a killer here!"

"I know." Her expression turned sympathetic which only infuriated me more. "But you are usually more thorough and you have more evidence than a vague suspicion." She turned to Makawee. "Would you please wake Kele? I believe Sister Dawn Star is attending him at the moment."

"Yes, m'lady," the head of household murmured. She bowed and retreated to the doorway to the second floor stairs.

"Who do you propose for the truthspell?" I said, barely keeping my temper in check.

"What about Brother Elu?" Mya inclined her head toward the Death priest. "Unless you prefer someone else." She shrugged. "However, you seem to think time is of the essence."

"Fine." I looked at the brother. "I want the matter settled before I send half of Orrin's clergy and wardens on a wild hare chase."

A few moments later, Makawee reappeared with Sister Dawn Star and Kele.

"Sit down, Kele." I gestured at the nearest bench. "We need to have a little talk."

A hopeful expression appeared on his face "Did you find my daughter's murderer?"

"The chief justice is under the impression you killed her," Mya said.

"What?" Kele looked from Mya to me and back to the high sister. "Why would I report her missing if I killed her?" he asked with an incredulous expression.

"To steal her remains for nefarious purposes," I said.

The farmer stiffened, his color turned an angry red, and an outraged expression filled his face. "How dare you—"

I took a step closer. "I dare because I am the chief justice of Orrin, and it is my duty to uphold the law and exact punishment where it is due."

Mya rested her palm on his shoulder. "Don't worry, Kele. Brother Elu will be the one who casts the truthspell. The chief justice will ask you questions. And I will be here to make sure the law is followed to the letter." She said the last with a pointed look at me.

My blood boiled at her insinuation.

You did kill that renegade last winter with your truthspell, the voices reminded me.

I ignored them. If the idiot hadn't tried to withhold the truth, he'd still be alive. It wasn't my fault he didn't have the good sense to commit suicide via poison like every other renegade or Assassins Guild member I'd run into.

"Have a seat," Brother Elu repeat Mya's command. "As long as you tell the truth, nothing will happen to you. If you don't know the answer to the chief justice's question, say 'I don't know.' Naiveté is not illegal."

"A-all right." Kele lowered himself to the bench.

Elu straddled the bench, facing the farmer. "Is this your first truthspell?"

Kele nodded.

"The spell will feel warm." Elu smiled. "To some people, it may feel like a tickle or a tingle on your skin."

I couldn't contain my anger. "Quit coddling him, and do the damn spell!"

Mya stepped between me and the farmer. "This is not Balance, and you will not treat our citizens thusly."

Elu murmured something I didn't catch. Magic crawled against my skin. The feel of Death talent was somewhere between the coziest cotton quilt and earthworms oozing along your palm. I would have preferred a Light priest, but I managed to break all of them except Sister Shi Hua, and she had the stupid breeding edict inhibiting her.

"May I question him now that the brother has cast the truthspell?" Sarcasm dripped from my voice.

Mya stepped aside. Only then, did I notice her palm gripped her dagger. Did she really consider drawing on me?

Only if you make me, Anthea. Her mental voice flittered like butterfly wings in my mind. But then, some species of butterflies consumed human flesh.

I pulled a bench closer to the one Kele and Elu sat on and perched on it. Calming my mind, I ripped through the basic questions establishing Kele's identity, occupation, and residence. One of my clerks should be present to record his answers, but I didn't want to waste the time to fetch one of them here.

"Have you ever eaten human flesh?" I said, getting to the meat of my questions. The voices tittered at my pun.

"No!" Kele started to rise. "What in the Twelve kind of question is that?"

Elu laid a hand on Kele's arm. "She's doing her job. You saw what was left of Pavati. Please, let her finish." However, Elu looked at me with an appalled expression.

It didn't matter. The questions needed to be answered. "Did you kill Pavati?"

"No!" Kele's skin grew even more red, if that was possible, but it was his rage that pounded against my mental shields.

"Did you sell her to anyone?"

"No."

"Did you leave the Temple of Child between Brother Elu escorting you here last night until my arrival this morning?"

"No," Kele ground out.

I continued asking him the same questions, rewording them to try to catch him, but he shouted his answers until he was hoarse. Not once did Elu's truthspell waver.

Mya was right.

Kele was innocent.

Chapter 20

I was so, so wrong in my suspicions. The voices found my mistake hysterically funny. I wanted to scream, but I needed to keep my composure.

Slowly, I pushed to my feet. "Thank you for your time, Farmer Kele. You may dissolve the truthspell, Brother Elu."

The ooze of Death magic disappeared.

"Does this mean you'll look for the real killer now, Chief Justice?" Kele stood to look me in the eye. "Or are you going to question every other innocent person in Orrin?"

"Watch your tongue, Farmer." I stepped closer until we were chest-to-chest. "You are not beyond a lashing for defying a Temple seat."

"That's enough," Mya snapped. She inserted herself between Kele and me by driving her elbow into my ribs. As thin as she was, the joint in question was exceptionally sharp. I suppose I should have been glad she decided to forgo her dagger. "Don't you have people waiting for you at the Wildling Temple, Chief Justice?"

"Yes, I do." What I would have preferred was to crawl back under my covers from dawn to dawn. I was so tired of everyone else's anger when I was just trying to perform my duties and keep them safe.

Instead, I pivoted on my boots and marched for the main doors of Child. I could have sworn the burning sensation at the back of my head was Mya's glare, but I didn't have the energy to turn around and see for certain.

When I reached Wildling, an excited hum came from inside. I entered to find Xander standing near the statue of the Wildling God with Jax, Han, Leocadia, Talbert, and DiCook. As one, they turned to look at me.

The hum of conversation died when the rest of the clergy and wardens sitting on the risers followed the line of sight of the seats and the magistrate. So, we were back to everyone staring at me like I was a demon.

Or an omen of evil.

I approached the group standing near the statue's dais. "Kele isn't our culprit after all. He spent the night at Child. High Sister Mya and her staff all confirm his story."

"So, where does that leave us?" Leocadia asked. "Do we try the tracking spell on the shard of claw we cleared?"

"We don't have a choice." Jax stated as he held out his hand to me. "Chief Justice?"

I resisted the urge to groan. "It's still in my office."

"It's a little hard to track a monster if we don't have the necessary ingredients for a tracking spell." Han grinned, but his jovial manner only added fuel to the fire of my anger.

"I'm sorry I haven't fulfilled all your needs, High Brother," I snapped.

His huge, bushy blue beard twitched. "What the demon is wrong with you, Anthea?"

"Wrong?" I growled. "I'm wrong? Because the Red Justice can't keep anyone safe?" Everyone in the Wildling sanctuary stared at me. I was so tired of being the center of everyone's attention, too.

"Chief Justice, why don't I walk with you to Balance?" DiCook gestured toward the double doors. He was smart enough not to touch me. If he did, I would have sliced his hand from his body.

He matched my pace as we left the Wildling Temple and headed up the thoroughfare to Balance. Noko continued to follow me silently.

"Have you taken a look at the witness reports about Barbora's shop my peacekeepers took on Second Day?" DiCook asked.

"When have I had time to do so?" I bit out.

"Fair enough, but if you suspected Kele of killing his daughter, you might want to look at the reports before you cast the tracking spell." He glanced at me. "I think you're right, and the creature danced right through Orrin's gates while in human form."

"They've been delivered to my clerks and translated to Balance code?"

"They were delivered to your Temple yesterday morning." He shrugged. "I can't vouch for Donella or Leilani's speed in translating them."

"But the bodies . . ."

Gorge rose in my throat. What if the wechuge had a way to keep the victims under control before it ate them? Like if the victims were frozen and close to death, but not dead?

I picked up my pace and took the steps of Balance two at a time.

Warden Long Feather nodded as my little group approached and opened the right door for me. I charged through the inner doors into the court room.

Elizabeth, Little Bear, and the clerks looked toward me. Though Elizabeth couldn't see me, she could hear my bootsteps, and her mind brushed mine.

"What's wrong?" she asked brusquely.

"The peacekeepers delivered the witness statements yesterday," I said. "I need them even if they haven't been translated yet."

Leilani rose. "I did get them translated, m'lady. I'll fetch them from your desk." She raced out of the courtroom in the direction of my office.

"Did you find Kele?" Elizabeth asked.

"Yes, but he's not our murderer."

Elizabeth cocked her head. "You thought he was the culprit?"

"I . . . suspected, but I just questioned him," I said. "He was at Child when Death was attacked."

I fidgeted and paced. What was taking Leilani so long?

My junior clerk rushed in with a sheaf of parchment connected by a brass tack. "Here it is, m'lady."

I took the sheaf from her and perched on a nearby bench. My fingertips drifted across the parchment. I paused on the statement by Mistress Jaci's youngest sister and looked at DiCook.

"The peacekeepers asked Moema about any missing people from Redwood Grove?"

"We've learned a lot from you."

"Balance!" I swore. "She told Peacekeeper Leyti she left the village well after Kele said search parties went out for Pavati from both Redwood Grove and Eagle Reach. There isn't any reason she wouldn't have known the girl was missing."

"True." He stroked his beard. "She probably counted on the girl being reported to Justice Erato when she came through Eagle Reach."

I turned to my senior clerk. "Donella, when is—"

"Justice Erato is scheduled to be here a fortnight after the Vintner's Festival," she said. "Depending on how long she and Brother Wolf Run take to resupply and file their reports—"

"Twelve help us." I groaned. "We weren't supposed to know about this for a couple of months."

"Surely, she had to have known the death of Brother Caleb would have been reported to Wildling," Elizabeth said.

"Eventually." I shook my head. "But does anyone in Eagle Reach realize Caleb was murdered? Kele didn't."

"Correct me if I'm wrong, Chief Justice, but if the creature uses demon magic, it's going to know you've cast the tracking spell, even if you seats clear that backlash magic from its body parts, right?" DiCook said.

I swallowed hard. "Yes."

Dizziness swept through me. I'd stood right next to the creature two days ago and didn't even recognize it.

Chapter 21

I ran my fingers over the statements once again to be sure. I was such an idiot. The wechuge had been inside Orrin's walls this whole time.

I looked up at DiCook. "We still have the issue of destroying it."

He frowned. "Brother Garbhan put in a research request at Knowledge. They haven't found with anything yet?"

"No." I chewed on my lip as I considered my options.

You know how to destroy it, the voices whispered. *Do it before it consumes us all.*

I opened my mouth to say something. Something that would result in me losing my head, but I couldn't let the wechuge kill anyone else. The voices' howls swirled through my mind in their impotent rage.

"Elizabeth, there's something you should know—"

"Chief Justice Anthea!" a male voice shouted.

Little Bear's sword sang from its scabbard, and he nearly sliced the brother from Knowledge in half. Luckily, Noko yanked the idiot priest out of the way.

DiCook laughed outright. "Brother Luca, have you heard none of the gossip about Balance in the last year? The wardens here stab first and ask questions later."

"A lesson that almost led to the magistrate's own throat getting sliced the other morning for doing the exact same thing." My head stopped

140

pounding now that the voices realized I wasn't going to betray them this instant. "What is it, Brother Luca?"

"We found something, but it's not an exact match." He gulped in air since Noko still had a firm grip around his neck.

"Let the boy go, Warden Noko," Elizabeth said. "He can't tell Anthea his news if he can't breathe."

Noko released him while Little Bear sheathed his sword.

Brother Luca rubbed his throat before he began. "According to myths of the Algonquin Nation, there's a creature called the wendigo. A human cursed for becoming a cannibal. There's different ways to kill it. A silver knife through the heart. Cut out the heart and melt it. Cut the body up with a silver-plated ax. The one thing in common in all the stories is you have to be fast because it heals almost immediately."

"What if we burn the whole body?" I asked.

"It should work." Brother Luca shrugged. "However, I can't guarantee anything."

"That's good enough for me," I said.

"How are you going to burn it if the damn thing melts?" DiCook asked. "The water will put out any fire."

"Then we're going to have to find a way to burn it without fire." My method may destroy what was left of our Light clergy, and I shuddered at the thought.

Fortunately, I had a good silversmith under contract. While Master Govind didn't have any silver-plated axes, he did have a ceremonial silver knife he hadn't quite finished.

I grinned at him. "How did you know I would need one?"

A wry smile crossed his face. "I didn't. It's supposed to be a wedding present from Lady Aurora to her groom at the Vintner's Festival."

I handed him three gold crowns. "Her husband just died six months ago." At the Battle of Tandor, but I couldn't bring myself to say those words.

Govind shrugged. "Nobles." He packed a lot of meaning into that one word. If I had time, I would have asked him.

"Send her to me if she gives you any trouble," I said.

"I'll have another made for her before the wedding." He nodded toward the knife as I slipped it into my left wrist sheath. "That isn't going to stand up in a real fight, m'lady."

"I'll tell you what it's for later," I said as I mounted Nassa. With a command, she trotted in the direction of the Merchant District.

Less than half a candlemark later, clergy and wardens surrounded Mistress Jaci's home, a townhouse with a garden in the back. She lived in one of the nicer parts of the city since her husband was a captain of one of Duke Marco's merchant ships, and Jaci herself own three seamstress shops. The building was definitely big enough to hold her, her sisters, and all their children.

DiCook's peacekeepers managed to quietly clear the neighbors on either side of Jaci's home while I dealt with Master Govind the silversmith. If Moena could bend the iron on the city gates, I wanted civilians out of the way.

Little Bear watched my back while I knocked on the front door.

One of the girls answered. Her eyes widened, and she quickly dropped a curtsey. "Welcome to our home, Lady Justice. Please come in. I'll get my mother."

After we entered and the girl closed the door, she hurried toward the back of the house.

Tapestries hung from the walls, and fine-carved furniture decorated the visiting room, but I couldn't tell much more beyond that. A moment passed, then Jaci and her sisters entered. The eldest Maiara scowled at me, much as she had two mornings ago. Moema had a pleasant expression fixed to her face, which made me even more nervous.

Jaci's expression though was hopeful. "Please tell me you have good news for us, Chief Justice."

"Actually, I need to ask all of you some questions under truthspell." I tried to project an apologetic smile. "Another witness has come forward and says you and your family placed the limbs in the shop. Unfortunately, you've admitted you had the keys during the same time period."

Jaci blinked rapidly and confusion filled her lovely face. "But you did a rewind, m'lady. You know it wasn't any of us."

"The truthspell is a formality." I waved my hand nonchalantly.

"Didn't you question the other witness under a truthspell?" Maiara gestured violently. "If they say we did it, and we say we didn't, then what good is your magic?"

Part of me wanted to laugh. She hadn't even noticed we lacked a Light priest, much less any other clergy, for a formal questioning.

I shrugged. "It leads to the third alternative that one of you may know the culprit who did place the limbs there. And I'd have to question you under the truthspell to establish not only none of you did it, but also that you don't know who did." I gestured at the couch and chairs. "Moema, would you—"

She moved faster than I would have thought possible. Talons of ice raked across my abdomen. If I hadn't jumped back, my guts would have spilled across Jaci's pristine floorboards.

Moema backhanded Little Bear before his sword cleared its sheath. He slammed into the wall and dropped to the floor. I couldn't tell if he was stunned or worse. I drew the silver knife. My goal was to get Moema into the garden.

Meanwhile, Maiara started screaming in raw panic. Jaci kept her head, drew her utility knife, and moved to cover her older sister. She gave me the opening to slip past Moena who was shifting and growing. Frigid air rolled off the wechuge as I darted past her, slicing her back as I went.

The wechuge screeched, a high-pitched sound that pained my ears. The wound slowed her enough, but her talons raked the back of my robes into ribbons. I yanked the ties loose with my free hand and flung the heavy cloth onto the thing's horns.

I reached the garden. The daughters cowered against the far wall. One shook the handle to the gate in a desperate attempt to get away, but Talbert had already cast a spell to freeze the lock.

The wechuge bellowed, this time in fury. I whirled to face the creature, and it charged through the back door of the townhouse, taking a good chunk of the surrounding bricks with it. What was left of my robes dangled from one horn.

Light magic tingled against my skin. With a series of *thunks*, arrows buried themselves in the wechuge's frozen hide. This time, High Mother Leocadia and Sister Claudia charged their weapons with their alternate talents. Garbhan and Jeremy stood with the two women on the neighboring roofs, also with bows in their hands.

The wechuge screamed again. Instead of arrowheads melting its flesh until they were no longer embedded and falling to the ground, flames licked its body. I took a running start, leapt, and plunged the silver dagger into its chest. There was a sharp *crack*, and we tumbled across the flagstones.

When I came to a rest on the flagstones, there was nothing but the crackle and pop of the magical flames consuming the ice. I rose to my hands and knees, then forced myself to my feet. Drops of my blood had splattered over the stones and plants, but the wechuge was perfectly still.

"Are you all right, Anthea?" Leocadia called.

"Nothing a healer can't fix," I yelled back. Or I hoped they could. The tears across my abdomen had ruined my uniform shirt, and the skin beneath the ruined silk was numb.

I took one step toward the wechuge's corpse when someone screamed as they plowed into my back.

Chapter 22

I landed on the dead wechuge and rolled with the blow to keep from catching my own clothes and hair on fire. The stink of scorched leather and silk filled my nose despite the fact that my tunic was soaked with melting wechuge. I didn't look forward to Sivan's complaints over my ruining of another uniform.

Coming to a rest against a wall, I looked over at the corpse. Another wechuge stood over it. I blink tears and blood from my eyes. This one had more green than blue and purple to its body, which meant it was warmer.

By the gate, the other girls stared at the second wechuge in soundless panic. Then I realized there was one less girl than before.

Two of them. That explained why the solid talon was imbedded in the victim's femur. The girl hadn't completely transformed yet like Moema had.

Before I could regain my feet, the new wechuge charged across the courtyard, snagged my ankle and tossed me. The cold penetrated my boot. That was my only thought before I landed on a bench, snapping the wood.

I saw blur of green and twisted away from it. The wechuge's blow finished what was left of the bench.

Anthea, get away from that thing, Leocadia shouted inside my head.

We don't have a clear shot. The demon voices were screaming the same thing.

Shoot it anyway, I said silently as I tried to somersault away and draw my sword. *It'll kill me if you don't.*

An arrow whistled over my head and cracked the tip of the second wechuge's left horn. We needed the silver knife to finish it.

I gained my feet and backslashed blindly. My sword struck something solid and there was another *crack*. But instead of the expected shriek of pain, the wechuge simply laughed, a noise reminiscent of shaking bits of ice in a glass goblet. I completed my spin to find one wechuge hand on the ground, melting, while another hand grew from the wechuge's stump.

A volley of Light magic-enhanced arrows forced the wechuge away from me. I turned and raced for the other wechuge's corpse. The fingers of my left hand wrapped around the hilt of the silver knife when the living wechuge grabbed my leg again.

This time it was above my boot, and my leggings did little to protect me from the cold. Numbness ran from toes to thigh. All it had to do was squeeze. My leg bones would snap and I would be helpless.

I concentrated and yanked time to a stop. I twisted and plunged the silver knife in the second wechuge's chest. I couldn't keep my grip on time. It clicked forward.

The second wechuge howled and dropped me. My sword clattered across the flagstones. I landed with a meatier sound. Another volley of magic-charged arrows struck the creature and it tumbled to the ground.

I raised my head a bit. The first wechuge looked like nothing more than a pile of melting snow. Steeling myself against the pain, I climbed to my feet and stumbled over to the first wechuge. I looked over at the girls huddled by the gate.

"Go inside the house," I ordered. When they didn't move, I roared, "Now!"

The girls scrambled for the hole Moema left in the back of the building, keeping as far from me as physically possible.

The rage and grief at the senseless deaths built inside of me until the lightning exploded.

Chapter 23

I passed out for a few moments after I evaporated the remains of the two wechuge with lightning. I didn't like the dark emotions I needed to feel to summon it. The damn voices cheered at the lightning that destroyed the remains of their enemy.

Thankfully, Little Bear was all right though the healers treated him for a concussion. His injury kept Sivan distracted from my ruined uniform. For now.

From what we could piece together from Moema's surviving daughter, Moema had gone to her own mother's cabin last winter to care for the elderly woman who was sick. A blizzard trapped her at the cabin for nearly a month. When Moema returned to her own home, all she told the daughters was that their grandmother had died, and Moema said she disposed of the body. A few days later, she sent her daughters to Jaci. A part of Moema was still human enough she didn't want to eat her own children.

The girl admitted Moema had arrived several days earlier than either Jaci or Maiara knew. Moema and her eldest daughter spent a great deal of time alone for those days. Garbhan was sure it was the daughter he and Noko had witnessed at the shop. We had no idea if Moema tricked the girl into eating human flesh or she did so willingly, but there was no doubt the daughter ate the five victims to accelerate her transformation into a full-fledged wechuge.

Given that the doors to the shop were locked, it appeared that the eldest daughter stole the key from Jaci to go in and out. Was she just stupid, or did she think this was the safest place to devour her victims?

Warden Gina suggested Moema and her daughter wanted to sabotage the shop in order to claim it from Maiara and her daughters. Whatever the case, Jaci had High Mother Leocadia perform a cleansing ritual against any remaining wechuge influences. Jaci and her family planned to clean the place thoroughly and allow High Brother Xander to destroy anything stained with blood and other bodily fluids.

High Brother Jax's second Farrah and her team of wardens found the missing limbs buried in the Wildling Grove outside of the city walls. High Brother Xander wasted no time in burning the remains.

Where Moema and her eldest learned demon magic was a question no one could answer. The younger daughter ended up in Mya's care after she realized her mother had no choice but to transform her into a wechuge, too, or kill her.

Jaci had already filed a petition to adopt her surviving niece. I prayed to Balance she knew what she was getting into.

I finished stamping out my report to the Reverend Mother. It detailed everything except the voices and the grimoire. Everything in my body ached except the slices across my abdomen. Those burned. I refused to be healed. If I was, I would be useless for the next fortnight. For once, all the master healers agreed with me, and Bly let her apprentice Simi use me for suture practice.

Leaving the parchment in the box for Donella to make copies, I pushed to my feet and padded out of my office. I hadn't bothered with a uniform. Instead, I'd pulled on some loose, clean exercise clothes. The tunic and pants didn't rub against the bandages the way my uniform did.

I headed out to our garden to clear my head before I retired to my quarters for some sleep. However, my desire for peace was short-lived.

Nathan and Ming Wei raced out of the stable before I could reach my favorite bench. They altered their course the moment they spotted me.

"Tell us about the monsters you killed!" Nathan's excitement grated along my psyche.

"After you have finished your chores," I said.

"We did, m'lady. Nassa and all the horses have been curried, combed, watered, and fed."

Ming Wei nodded along with Nathan's words.

"Can we hear about the monster?" he asked earnestly.

"They weren't monsters," I said. Irritation crawled along my skin inside as well as out. "They were people caught in circumstances beyond their control."

"But Hogarth said—" Nathan began.

"I don't care what Hogarth said!" I shouted. "Just shut up!"

Nathan blinked and yellow tears gathered in his eyes. "I-I'm sorry, Lady Justice. I just wanted—"

"I said shut up!" My left hand rose to backhand the irritating, smelly nuisance.

"Leave him alone!" Ming Wei charged and shoved me. Right in the stitched cuts. Burning pain swept through my body, and I gasped for breath as I landed on my buttocks.

My sight shifted. I looked up.

Nathan was gone. All the colors were wrong. It was like seeing through Luc or one of my wardens' eyes.

A woman stood over me. She was tall with black hair hanging loose. She wore green robes and held a flaming sword in her right hand. Despite looking older, I knew her. The biggest thing was the awful scars on the left side of her face were gone.

I swallowed hard.

"Ming Wei?"

Chapter 24

"What is wrong with you?" Ming Wei shouted. "You know better than to strike a child—" Her attention shifted, and she stared at something behind me. "Oh, no."

We were no longer in the Balance garden, but on a grassy plain. I climbed to my feet, my pain gone. I was dressed in my Balance uniform and robes. When I turned to look, my own heart threatened to leap out of my throat.

Demons. I was seeing demons how they looked in their true form to normally sighted humans. Except something was wrong. They looked cadaverous. They seethed and slithered, but they didn't approach.

As if they weren't sure what was going on either.

"No wonder you've been acting weirdly," Ming Wei murmured.

"Where—" I swallowed, but my mouth remained dry. "Where are we?"

She chuckled. "I believe we're inside your mind."

"B-but how—"

"I had to save Nathan," she murmured. "He's my first friend."

I shivered at what I'd been about to do. She was right. I did know better. "How do we get out?"

She inclined her head toward the demons. "We need to destroy them first. Or you are going to get worse, Lady Justice."

"No!" the demons shouted together. "Destroy her! She'll kill you once we are gone. You know your own laws."

An ugly feeling of familiarity washed through me. The rotting demons were the visual representation of the voices in my head. And they were right. I would be executed for keeping their grimoire in my possession.

Because I couldn't kill Ming Wei even though she learned my secret.

A grin split my face as I looked at her. "I can slow them. Can you handle that sword?"

She glanced at the flaming weapon. "I always have before in my dreams."

"Go for the heads."

As one, we charged the demons. I cast a spell to slow time.

Ming Wei killed the first two quickly. I stabbed one and kicked back another. Then my spell failed. Claws raked across my abdomen in the same place where the wechuge had cut me. But this time, my intestines spilled out.

If we died inside my mind, we would die in real life. And no one would know to destroy the grimoire before it was too late.

I clamped one arm against the burning pain and swung my sword. It loped off the head of the demon about to stab Ming Wei in the back.

We stood shoulder to shoulder, then back to back.

"You need to fry them, Anthea!" she shouted.

"What?"

"Call the lightning!"

Horror washed through me. "What if I do it in real life? It'll kill you and Nathan."

She laughed, a wild sound that echoed across the plain. "You won't. Do it!"

I let go of the rage and guilt and fear. Light flashed, and the sharp crack of thunder filled my ears.

And then I was falling. Falling into a black pit.

A hand shot out and grabbed mine.

"Let go, child!" I screamed. "I'll drag you in, too!"

This time, her laughter sounded more like the little girl giggles she let out when she thought no adults were around. "Someone's got me, and I have you. There's too much to do to let you fall."

Chapter 25

I woke up in chains. Spell-threaded chains. Ming Wei had told everyone the truth. She saved me only for me to lose my head.

Except I wasn't wearing the roughspun tunic of someone in the Balance gaol. Instead, the tunic was soft cotton. I lay on a pallet. Carefully, I rolled into a sitting position. My stitches tugged and pulled, but I only had the cuts the wechuge had inflicted. The walls were padded, oiled leather as was the floor when I reached out. I was in Child. One of the cells for someone so mad, they feared the person would hurt themselves or someone else.

With the rattling of my chains, footsteps sounded in the corridor outside of my cell. Whoever was out there was walking away. Maybe they kept watch long enough to know I was alive.

I lay back down. For the first time in months, utter silence rang in my head. I just prayed the grimoire hadn't gotten its claws into anyone else, and the other seats had the sense to destroy the damn book.

I was such a fool to believe I could handle that thing and not come away unscathed. Maybe this was how Balance leveled the scales. My life for unlocking Ming Wei's potential.

Footsteps echoed outside my cell. This time they came closer. The lock rattled and the door swung open. I sat up again as Mya stepped inside.

"Why am I here?" I asked. "Elizabeth should have beheaded me on Ming Wei's testimony alone."

"You were soaked in wechuge fluids." Mya grimaced. "The Knowledge clergy were still digging while you dealt with the two in the city. According to them, close contact with a wendigo can transform a human into a wendigo, too. We surmise it's the same for wechuge. If you became one, you would have been useless to the demons."

"They tried to kill me and Ming Wei," I said.

"According to her, it was just you." Mya shrugged. "Your usefulness was gone, and they thought Yanaba's squire was damaged enough for them to twist." She smiled. "You both surprised them because you've turned your pain into strength."

"I wasn't strong enough to destroy the grimoire like I should have."

Mya sat on the padded leather floor and leaned against the wall opposite of me. She regarded me for a long time before she said, "You're not going to get what you want, Anthea."

"And what is that?"

"Death." She sighed and shook her head. "You've been suicidal since Chief Justice Thalia took you from Love."

"You have it wrong," I muttered. "Gerd sold me."

Mya ignored my statement. "Reverend Mother Alara admitted to my Reverend Mother she assigned Luc to you, hoping he could give you something to live for. It's the reason she ignored your relationship."

No, that couldn't be true. "He was told to seduce me?"

"No," Mya said. "He wasn't aware of the Reverend Mother's intention." She sighed again. "Instead of manipulating you, she should have referred you to the home Temple of Child for counseling. But she didn't, so we have a lot of work to do, you and I."

I ignored her challenge. I had a demon grimoire in my possession. The law was clear in the matter.

"Was the grimoire destroyed?"

"Yes, Luc and Claudia each assumed you'd destroyed it." Mya chuckled. "It wasn't until we all noticed your change in behavior over the last few weeks and compared notes that we realized the grimoire was still intact."

"I should be executed for not destroying it."

"The demons that formed the grimoire did things to your mind, Anthea. Executing you would be like executing Elizabeth or Luc for the crime of being tortured."

"I let them seduce me!" Hot tears burned my eyes.

Mya cocked her head. "Did you? Ming Wei said you fought them with her."

"Is she all right?" I asked softly.

"She's fine." Mya chuckled again. "In fact, the incident unlocked her talents, so there's no need for her to be tested."

I stared at the leather floor. "But she's so scared of leaving Balance."

"She locked up her talents as a way to protect herself from the abuse she endured," Mya said. "In a way, saving Nathan and you helped her own emotional equilibrium. I'll continue to work with her and train her. She's not ready to go to Standora yet. Maybe she never can, but she will have to register as a talent."

I looked up at Mya. "And me?"

"You're too valuable an asset, Anthea. It's why the renegades wanted you on their side. They realized their mistake in not recruiting you years ago. So they tried to do it through the grimoire. It's no mistake the book was smuggled out of Standora and given to Gerd. They knew she'd make a beeline to Orrin." Mya grinned. "Everyone in the Temples except Bianca placed their bets on you over Gerd. The renegades did to."

"You mean they manipulated me into getting rid of their problem."

"Yes," Mya admitted. "The question now is whether I can help you resume your duties."

"What if I don't want to?" I muttered sullenly.

"You're not the type to let a wrong go unavenged. Don't you want to find out who was behind making sure the grimoire messed with your mind?"

"Yes." I grinned at Mya. From the tightness of my muscles and skin, I knew it wasn't a very nice grin. "Yes, I do."

◈

If you are enjoying the adventures of Anthea and the people of the Justice universe, drop me a line through my website, www.suzanharden.com; on Twitter @Suzan_Harden or on Facebook at SuzanHardenWriter. Recommending the Justice series to your friends or writing a review would be even better.

The queen sends Chief Justice Anthea on a special diplomatic mission that takes her to Diné and a reunion with her biological father. Can Anthea face him again after beheading her own mother and nearly succumbing to the demon grimoire? Turn the page for a sneak peek of *A Hand of Father*!

A Hand of Father

Excerpt © 2021, Suzan Harden

The smell of Jing tea mixed with the dusty odor of old tomes in my office in the Temple of Balance. I stared at White Eagle, the Duke of Standora and the Lord General of the Queen's Army, who sat in a visitor chair on the other side of my desk.

"Are you jesting with me, sir?" I blurted.

"Do I look like I am joking, Chief Justice?" he said before scowling at me.

"B-but neither I nor High Brother Luc are in any shape to travel to Diné, much less lead a diplomatic delegation." I squeezed my cup, wishing the warmth of the ceramic would heat the bones of my hands. Ever since Squire Ming Wei pulled me from the brink of succumbing to demon magic, I constantly felt chilled. Not even sitting in the Temple kitchen while our cook Deborah baked could heat my body, much less my spirit.

"The Matriarch of the Diné requested you two specifically." A twitch of his lips wouldn't qualify as a smile on anyone else, but it was the closest the duke came to expressing any emotion. "Apparently, you two made an impression on their Reverend Father of Conflict."

I cleared my throat. It would be best to get things out in the open now, no matter how annoyed the duke may become.

"Are you aware the Reverend Father happens to be my biological sire, Your Grace?"

"Better him than me." The duke waggled his eyebrows. A full-fledged grin filled his face.

I stared at him. "This isn't funny."

"You are going, Chief Justice, and High Brother Luc will accompany you. That is a command from your orders' leaders and your queen." The duke saluted me with his cup. "End of discussion."

GLOSSARY

WORDS AND PHRASES SPECIFIC TO THE JUSTICE SERIES

Anacapa Islands – a series of four islands off the southwestern coast of Issura. Limuw is the largest. Wi'ma is the second largest. Anacapa is the closest to Orrin. Tuqan is the furthest from Orrin.

Apprentice – lowest rank of a trade or craft guild

Britannia – Toscan name for a series of islands off the western coast of the Old Continent. The two largest are Eire and Albion. Four hundred years before Anthea's time, the queens of Eire and Albion were losing their battle against the demons. They ordered the islands evacuated and the Temples of Death to launch their last resort spells. The islands are now barren, and no one who steps on them lives for long.

Briton Diaspora – refers to the survivors and their descendants of the evacuation of Britannia who are now scattered around the world

Brother – title for any fully ordained priest of any Temple that accepts men, except for the Temple of Father

Cant – Issura's neighboring nation-state to the south

Chengzhou – the capital of Jing, a nation-state in the western shore of the Old Continent

Chief Justice – title of the highest ranked priestess at a Temple of Balance

Chief [name of trade] – the highest ranking master guild member of a trade in a city or region

The Cradle – according to legend, the continent where Child created the first members of the human race

Duke/Duchess – highest ranking noble of a region

Distance-view glasses – a telescope

Father – title for any fully ordained priest of the Temple of Father

Gilwas – a city in northern Issura

Gray Mountains – a mountain range that runs the entire length of the western side of the Long Continents

The Grand Canal – a human-built canal that passes through the isthmus connecting the Long Continents

The Green Lady Inn – an inn near the Embassy District of Orrin, it had the only entrance/exit to the tunnel system with the city wall that is not a Temple until it was bricked over and magically sealed after the events of *A Modicum of Truth* and *A Matter of Death*.

Guild – a civil organization for a trade or craft

161

Guild Master – an expert tradesman's rank based on analysis of his/her peers

Healer – a person with the magical ability to heal illness and repair wounds

High Brother – title of the chief priest of a city Temple, except the Temple of Father

High Father – title of the chief priest of a city's Temple of Father

High Mother – title of the chief priestess of a city's Temple of Mother

High Sister – title of the chief priestess of a city Temple, except the Temples of Balance or Mother

Iberia – nation-state on the southwestern corner of the Old Continent

Issura – queendom on the western coast of Northern Long Continent; the Peaceful Sea forms its western border with the nation of Pagonia to the north, the nation of Cant to the south, the nations of the Cliffdwellers and Diné to the southeast and the Gray Mountains to the east

Jing – nation-state on the eastern side of the Old Continent

Journeyman/Journeywoman – middle rank of a trade or craft guild

Justice – title for any fully ordained priestess of the Temple of Balance; alternate term of address is Lady Justice

Kemet – nation-state on the northeast corner of the Cradle

The Levant – a loose alliance of Phoenician city-states between the Hittite Empire and Kemet on the eastern side of the Middle Sea

The Long Continents – the two continents separating the Peaceful Sea from the Panthalassa Sea, they are connected by a narrow isthmus

The Lost Continent – southern continent between the Peaceful Sea and the Storm Sea. By Anthea's time, the original inhabitants were believed to be slaughtered by demons 500 years before. Sailors from the Sea Peoples and Maurya who landed there after the inhabitants' disappearance reported screams but found no one. Those with magic talents went mad. Not even the priests and priestesses from Child could save them. Those who tried went mad themselves.

Magistrate – elected official of a city or town in Issura who is responsible for civil and criminal law enforcement and the city or town's defense/care in an emergency

Master – senior member of a trade or craft guild; the clergyperson who is primarily responsible for the training of a novice class

Maurya – the southern-most nation of the Old Continent

Middle Sea – shallow sea that separate The Cradle from the Old Continent

Mother – title for any fully ordained priestess of the Temple of Mother

National Road – main, paved road through the nation of Issura. It roughly parallels the western coastline.

New Thenos – an island city/state on the eastern coast of the Northern Long Continent

Novice – a person in training to become a priest/priestess of the Twelve

Orrin – third largest city in the queendom of Issura with the second largest port

Pagonia – Issura's neighboring nation to the north

Panthalassa Sea – ocean that separates the Long Continents from the western part of the Old Continent and the Cradle

Peaceful Sea – ocean that separates the Long Continents from the eastern part of the Old Continent, the islands and archipelagos of the Sea Peoples, and the Lost Continent

Peacekeepers – men and women who act as a city's police force. They report to the city's magistrate. They also act as an auxiliary defense force if their city or nation is attacked.

Pimu – one of a series of four island off the northern coast of Cant

Rambla – a city in northern Cant, its people were used to hatch demon eggs off-screen during the events of *A Modicum of Truth*

Reverend Father – senior-most priest of a Temple order, the leader of that sect in the nation in which he resides

Reverend Mother – senior-most priestess of a Temple order, the leader of that sect in the nation in which she resides

Seat – person holding the highest ranking position of a Temple

Shakya – nation-state in the western portion of the Old Continent, southwest of Jing and northeast of Maurya

Sister – title for any fully ordained priestess of any Temple that accepts women, except for the Temples of Mother and Balance

Standora – capital and largest city of Issura

Storm Sea – ocean bordered by the eastern part of the Cradle, the southern part of the Old Continent, and the western part of the Lost Continent

Tandor – Issuran city that guards the border with Cant and Diné

Temple – a collection of people dedicated to the service of one of the twelve gods; a building that houses such people; the primary place of worship for one of the twelve gods

Tiwan – the capital of Cant

Toscana – nation-state on the southwest section of the Old Continent; location of the first battle against the demons

The Twelve – the collective name for the twelve deities of the Justice universe

Valencia – duchy in the nation-state of Iberia; know for their innovative shipbuilding designs

Warden – security guard of a Temple, they act as supplementary military personnel in the event of a demon invasion

Mother

Cloak Color – Light blue

Motto – "To give without thought; to forgive with love."

The Temple of Mother is responsible for the teaching of household arts, such as spinning, weaving, food storage and preparation. The order is also responsible for caring for those who have lost their families.

Father

Cloak Color – Dark blue

Motto – "All tools are weapons, and weapons tools."

The Temple of Father is responsible for the constructive arts, such as carpentry and smithing.

Balance

Cloak Color – Black

Motto – "Balance in all things."

The Temple of Balance runs the judicial system. A justice is the judge in criminal and civil cases.

Light

Cloak Color – Medium brown

Motto – "Light brings truth, for without truth, there can be no justice."

The Temple of Light is responsible for codifying contracts and mediating contract disputes. A Light priest also acts as the bailiff for a justice, and is often the one to truthspell a witness or the accused. The Temple of Light also provides military support to a nation's civilian army.

Knowledge

Cloak Color – Gold

Motto – "With patience, knowledge comes."

The Temple of Knowledge is responsible for education and for recording historical events. They essentially act as the library system for the Justice universe.

Thief

Cloak Color – Grey

Motto – "Hiding in plain sight."

The Temple of Thief acts as the intelligence-gathering arm of both the Temples and the civilian leaders. They finance their efforts through gambling dens.

Conflict

Cloak Color – Dark Red

Motto – "Destruction is the necessary evil, for it clears the way for new growth."

The Temple of Conflict focuses on strategy and all martial arts. They are the primary support and teachers of a nation's army.

Love

Cloak Color – Medium Red

Motto – "Pleasure is life."

The Temple of Love are the holy prostitutes. They also deal with sex education and lead the Spring Rituals, the annual fertility rites which were first used to breed as many humans with magical talent as possible. Don't underestimate them. They fight just as hard and as nasty as their fellow clergy in Conflict.

Child

Cloak Color – Light green

Motto – "All things are new once."

The Temple of Child is responsible for the emotional health of citizens. They also develop and teach agriculture and animal husbandry techniques.

Wilding

Cloak Color – Dark green

Motto – "All creatures return to us."

The Temple of the Wildling God deals with management of wild animal populations, forestry, and the protection of ecosystems.

Vintner

Cloak Color – Purple

Motto – "The line between wisdom and madness is one sip."

The Temple of Vintner not only deals with the cultivation of grapes and the production of wine, but they also promote the gathering, cultivation and processing of all medicinal herbs.

Death

Cloak Color – Black

Motto – "For every life, there is a death."

The Temple of Death takes care of the gathering of the dead, the last rites, and disposal of the corpses. They also act as a repository for the last wills and testaments of all citizens.

Characters and Places

QUEENDOM OF ISURRA

ORRIN

Temple of Balance

Chief Justice Anthea – a circuit justice for ten winters until her appointment as Chief Justice of Orrin at the age of thirty winters ("Justice")

Chief Justice Penelope – deceased, predecessor to Anthea as Chief Justice of Orrin

Chief Justice Thalia – deceased, predecessor to Penelope as Chief Justice of Orrin, maternal grandmother to Anthea

Justice Yanaba – junior justice assigned to the city of Orrin after the events of *A Question of Balance*

Justice Erato – junior justice assigned to the circuit of the eastern section of the duchy of Orrin and the southern tip of the duchy of Pana Valley after Anthea is sentenced to the seat of Orrin in "Justice"

Sivan – personal assistant to Chief Justice Anthea and head of the household staff

Donella – senior clerk

Lailani – junior clerk

Chief Warden Little Bear – head of the Balance wardens

Warden Tyra – junior warden, killed in the Battle of Tandor (*A Matter of Death*)

Warden Gina – junior warden

Warden Aglaia – junior warden, died in the battle to retake the Temple of Love (*A Question of Balance*)

Warden Daniel – junior warden

Warden Noko – junior warden

Warden Jonata – junior warden, Aglaia's replacement from the Standora Wardens' Academy, a passive talent

Warden Dezba – junior warden

Warden Tahoma – junior warden

Warden Ahiga – junior warden

Warden Long Feather – junior warden

Warden Ailyn – junior warden, she replaced Tyra after her death

Warden Mylon – junior warden

Hogarth – former chief warden under Justices Thalia and Penelope, now stablemaster, husband of Deborah

Deborah – Head cook, wife of Hogarth

Nathan – squire to Chief Justice Anthea after he was sentenced to pay reparations for stealing bread, an orphan, age ten winters at the time of his sentencing in *A Question of Balance*

Ming Wei – squire to Justice Yanaba, nine winters old at the end of *A Question of Balance*. Originally from Jing, she was sold by her parents to a Jing noble as a sex slave and brought to Issura. When the noble's crimes were discovered, he immolated himself and his slaves. Ming Wei was the only survivor and has severe scar tissue on her face, back and arms.

Temple of Light

High Brother Luc – a circuit priest for twelve winters until his appointment as chief priest at the age of thirty-two winters between the events of "Justice" and "Diplomacy in the Dark"

High Brother Kam – semi-retired, predecessor to Luc as chief priest, poisoned and died during the events of *A Question of Balance*

Brother Mat – Second to Luc. His birth name is Micah. He murdered the real Mat on his way to Orrin from Standora. Died under Anthea's truthspell interrogation in *A Question of Balance*.

Brother Jeremy – youngest junior priest until he is promoted to Luc's second after the events of *A Question of Balance*.

Brother Garbhan – junior priest who is assigned permanently to Orrin after the events of *A Matter of Death*

Istaqa – personal assistant to High Brother Luc and head of the household staff

Edberth – former personal assistant to High Brother Kam, he now acts as evening assistant to High Brother Luc

Henry – stablemaster

Chief Warden Nicholas – head of the Light wardens

Warden Gibb – junior warden, died shortly after the renegades' kidnapping of High Brother Luc in *A Question of Balance*

Warden Mateqai – junior warden, becomes Sister Shi Hua's personal bodyguard during the events of *A Modicum of Truth*

Warden Yar – junior warden

Warden Tadhg – junior warden

Warden Gad – junior warden

Temple of Love

High Sister Gerd – chief priestess, biological daughter of Thalia and Kam, biological mother of Anthea. She was removed from office on charges of fraud, bribery of a public official, unlawful magic, and conspiracy to commit murder. Later, the charges of dealing in demon artifacts and treason were added.

Sister Dragonfly – Gerd's second, *berda* (genderfluid), is acting High Sister after the events in *A Question of Balance*, becomes High Sister after the events in *A Modicum of Truth*

Sister Gretchen – junior priestess, deceased. The discovery of her body in one of Duke Marco's wine barrels precipitates the events in *A Question of Balance*

Sister Claudia – junior priestess, Dragonfly's second

Sister Shada – junior priestess

Sister Zihna – junior priestess

Sister Ilina – junior priestess, Lady Katarina DiMara's mother, she died of the wasting disease prior to "Justice"

Chief Warden Citana – new chief warden of Love after renegades killed and replaced the entire warden contingent of the temple

Warden Jocasta – junior warden, one of the replacement wardens after the events of *A Question of Balance*

Gregorios – a eunuch who was High Sister Dragonfly's personal assistant and head of household until his murder prior to the beginning of *A Twist of Love*

Ichik – a eunuch who is Sister Claudia's personal assistant

Iona – Love's maintenance person, she does minor repairs and servicing of the Temple

Temple of Conflict

High Brother Han – chief priest

Sister Migina – junior priestess

Brother Pimu – junior priest

Temple of Death

High Sister Bertrice – chief priestess

High Brother Kai – deceased, predecessor of Bertrice, retired in Bertrice's favor as the temple seat and became a teaching brother in Standora until his death

Brother Xander – Bertrice's second until her demise during the Battle of Tandor, succeeds her as Orrin's High Brother of Death

Sister Raven Claw – Xander's second when he becomes high brother

Brother Elu – junior priest

Chief Warden Axton – head of the Death wardens

Warden Hitari – junior warden

Temple of Vintner

High Brother Ben – chief priest

Sister Nina – junior priestess

Chief Warden Mangas – head of the Vintner wardens

Warden Golden Eagle – junior warden, murdered by Gerd during the events of *A Twist of Love*

Temple of Mother

High Mother Bianca – chief priestess, she commits suicide when Anthea discovers Bianca has been selling children

High Mother Leocadia – chief priestess, she transferred from the Temple in Gilwas and succeeded Bianca between the events in *A Touch of Mother* and *A Twist of Love*

Chief Warden Maebh – head of the Mother wardens

Temple of Father

High Father Jerrod – chief priest

Temple of Child

High Sister Mya – chief priestess

Brother Turtle – junior priest, helps to save Justice Yanaba by pulling her soul back into her body during the events of *A Modicum of Truth*

Sister Dawn Star – junior priestess

Makawee – Child's head of household and Mya's personal assistant

Chief Warden High Rock – head of the Child wardens

Temple of Wildling

High Brother Jax – chief priest, second form is a wolf

Sister Farrah – Jax's second, second form is a fox

Temple of Thief

High Brother Talbert – chief priest

Sister Cedar Grove – Talbert's second

Chief Warden Sabine – head of the Thief wardens

Temple of Knowledge

High Sister Mariana – chief priestess

Brother Luca – junior priest

Nobility

Duke Benedetto DiMara – father of Marco, Alessa, and Isabella, husband of Cora, convicted of conspiracy and conspiracy for illegal magic to mind wipe his son Marco during the events of "Justice"; imprisoned at Standora for life.

Lady Cora DiMara – mother of Marco, Alessa, and Isabella, convicted of treason and demon dealing, executed by the Reverend Mother Alara of Balance during the events of "Justice".

Duke Marco DiMara – duke of Orrin, inherited his post at the age of eighteen winters after his parents were found guilty of numerous offenses and stripped of their titles and property

Lady Katarina DiMara (nee' DiLove) – common-born wife of Marco, animal healer. Her mother Sister Ilina was a priestess of the Temple of Love and died of the wasting sickness shortly before Katarina's eighteenth winter.

Lord Kam DiMara – eldest child of Marco and Katarina and heir to the Duchy of Orrin, named for High Brother Kam of Light, godson of Chief Justice Anthea and High Brother Luc

Lady Alessa DiMara – sister of Marco, a latent talent, lover of Sister Gretchen of Love

Lady Isabella DiMara – sister of Marco, attends the University of Standora

Bartholomew – retainer of Duke Marco's until it was learned he'd assaulted Lady Alessa and Sister Gretchen, Lady Alessa subsequently asked Chief Justice Anthea for clemency and hired him to manage the estates Sister Gretchen had bequeathed to Alessa

William – retainer of Duke Marco's

Julian – retainer of Duke Marco's

Arturo – former captain of Duke Marco's flagship, his murder is the precipitating event of "Diplomacy in the Dark"

Titus – captain of Duke Marco's flagship, the *Mars Tranquilus*

Citizens

Malven DiCook – duly elected magistrate of Orrin

Dante – one of Orrin's peacekeepers, dies at the beginning of *A Modicum of Truth*

Barbora – wife of Dante, dies at the beginning of *A Modicum of Truth*

Jaime – one of Orrin's peacekeepers

Leyti – one of Orrin's peacekeepers

Drest – a peacekeeper, dismissed by DiCook for extortion

Robin – a peacekeeper, dismissed by DiCook for warning Drest that DiCook was coming to arrest him

Alo – an innkeeper, the owner of the Green Lady Inn near the Embassy District

Chumana – Alo's daughter, she is ten winters at the beginning of *A Question of Balance*

Guilds

Chief Healer Aaron – head of the Healers' Guild

Master Healer Devin – second to Aaron in the Orrin Healer's Guild, originally from New Thenos

Journeywoman Bly – a junior healer, often assists Master Devin at autopsies, later a master healer in her own right

Simi – Bly's apprentice at the Healers Guild when Bly attains master status

Master Healer Una – a master healer who specializes in head trauma and sleep disorders, she also happens to be a dreamwalker

TANDOR

High Brother Dav – chief priest of the Temple of Light

Chief Justice Elizabeth – chief justice of the Temple of Balance

Minerva – the new clerk with the Temple of Balance, a renegade, killed during the fight within the Temple of Balance (*A Modicum of Truth*)

High Brother Aduba – chief priest of the Temple of Conflict

Brother Tighan – second of the Temple of Conflict, a renegade, killed by Aduba during the fall of Tandor

High Brother Nantan – chief priest of the Temple of Death

Sister Reby – second of the Temple of the Wildling God, first introduced as a shapeshifting thief in "The Perfect Partner", second form is a polecat

Brother Sisquoc – surviving priest of the Temple of the Wildling God, second form is a panther

Brother Trajan – priest of the Temple of the Wilding God, second form is a wolf

Sister Jumping Mouse – priestess of the Temple of the Wildling God, second form is a kangaroo rat

Duke Enzo DiToscana – Duke of Tandor, murdered by a skinwalker possessing his wife

Duchess Nadine DiToscana – the widow of Duke Enzo of Tandor

Ural DiSand – merchant from Tandor, implicated in the Assassin Guild plots in Orrin, killed while possessed by a skinwalker (*A Modicum of Truth*)

Amarantha DiRoma – Tandoran merchant, rival of Ural DiSand, murdered by renegades shortly before they poisoned most of the personnel of the Tandoran Temples

Govind – a silversmith who assisted with the defense of Tandor against the demon army, settled in Orrin after the evacuation and fall of Tandor

The Wave Dancer – Duchess Nadine of Tandor's flagship, one of two remaining ships in Tandor prior to the Battle of Tandor

STANDORA – capital city of Issura

Reverend Mother Alara – head of Issura's Temple of Balance

Justice Rose – novice training priestess of the main Temple of Balance in Standora when Anthea was a novice

Justice Melanippe – a novice in Anthea's class. She was the top student, but she was also recruited by Thief to report on any wrongdoing in Balance.

Reverend Father Farrell – head of Issura's Temple of Light

Brother Elroy – a Light priest, aide to Reverend Father Farrell, and a distance speaker who accompanies the Isurran and Sea Peoples' fleets to Tandor in *A Matter of Death*

Brother Long Wind – a Light priest and aide to Reverend Father Farrell; he accompanies the queen's army to Tandor in *A Matter of Death*

Brother Garbhan – a Light priest and aide to Reverend Father Farrell; he remains in Orrin during and after the events of *A Matter of Death*

Brother Jon – novice training priest at the main Temple of Light in Standora, murdered by the skinwalker at Samael DiRoy's abandoned manse prior to *A Question of Balance*

High Sister Imala – a Love priestess, considered to be the lead contender for position of Reverend Mother of Love; she accompanies the queen's army in A Matter of Death

Chief Warden Catherine – Imala's chief warden; she was a classmate of Mateqai's at the Warden Academy and the two had a physical relationship

Warden Hototo – a junior Love warden

Brother White Wolf – a senior priest of Thief; he's a personal friend of High Sister Imala

Queen Teodora – reigning monarch of Issura

Crown Princess Chiara – eldest child and heir of Queen Teodora of Issura; lady general of the queen's army

Duke White Eagle – former Conflict brother, left the order to marry Crown Princess Chiara; honorary title duke of Standora as the future queen's consort; lord general of the queen's army

PANA VALLEY

Lord Aleister DeGrove – noble noted for his vineyards

JING EMPIRE

CHENGZHOU

Empress Bao De – ruler of Jing a century before Bao Yu, she sacrificed herself to stop a demon army

Empress Bao Yu – ruler of Jing until her death from natural causes during "Courting Trouble"

Emperor Bao Chengwu – current ruler of Jing, succeeded his mother Bao Yu during "Courting Trouble"

Ambassador Quan Po – half-brother of the current Jing emperor Bao Chengwu; was heir to the throne until his nephew was born

Reverend Father Jin – head of Jing's Temple of Light

Sister Shi Hua – a priestess of Light, who was tapped as Po's bodyguard. She received additional training from Conflict, Thief, and Love. Originally from the town of Yintze in the southern province of Chu.

Brother Lin – novice master of Light

Brother Jian – a priest of Light, classmate of Shi Hua during their novice years

Brother Fa – a Wildling priest, his second form is a tiger, a friend of Shi Hua and Jian during their novice years

Justice Mei Wen – a priestess of Balance, Shi Hua's closest friend other than Jian during their novice years

Sister Yin Li – a priestess of Love, Shi Hua's maternal aunt

Yin Shang – the son of Sister Yin Li and Brother Shang

Reverend Father Chen – head of Jing's Temple of Conflict

Brother Shang – a priest of Conflict, Shi Hua's instructor when she was a novice

Reverend Father Biming – head of Jing's Temple of Thief

The Unbridled – a spy ship used by the Temple of Thief, a four-masted carrack built in the Iberian duchy of Valencia, captained by Reverend Father Biming during *A Modicum of Truth*

Brother Hadar – a priest of Thief from the Kingdom of Hejaz, serving on board *The Unbridled*

ISLANDS OF THE SEA PEOPLES

Kingdom of O'ahu

Prince Alika – youngest son of the king of the Sea Peoples, one of Sister Gretchen's worshippers, the father of her unborn child

Captain Iakepa – senior captain of the O'ahu trading fleet

DINÉ NATION

Reverend Father Nizhé'é' – head of the Diné Temple of Conflict

Justice Spotted Fawn – the western circuit justice for the Diné Nation, killed in the Battle of Tandor

Bidzii – Spotted Fawn's clerk, he's fluent in Issuran so the justice speaks through him; killed in the Battle of Tandor

Brother Bumblebee – junior priest of Light with the Diné army

Sister Lizard – junior priestess of Knowledge with the Diné army

CLIFFDWELLERS

Healer Kotori – a physician with the Diné army during the siege of Tandor

PLAINS NATIONS – COMANCHE

High Brother Pecos – a senior Conflict priest with the Diné army during the siege of Tandor

Acknowledgments

As always, much love and gratitude to Elaina Lee of For the Muse Design for her awesome cover and to Jaye Manus for making the interior design look so professional. Any typos are mine and mine alone;

To Bella the Princess Pup for keeping me company when I'm on a deadline;

And to my Darling Husband who held out Mexican food from my favorite place in town as a reward for meeting my deadline.

Suzan Harden transitioned from writing information technology manuals for companies and legal articles for a law enforcement magazine to her first love, fantasy and science fiction in all their forms. She's the author of the Bloodlines, the 888-555-HERO, and the Justice series.